Stone Hearts

A War of the Underhill Novella

S. E. Wendel

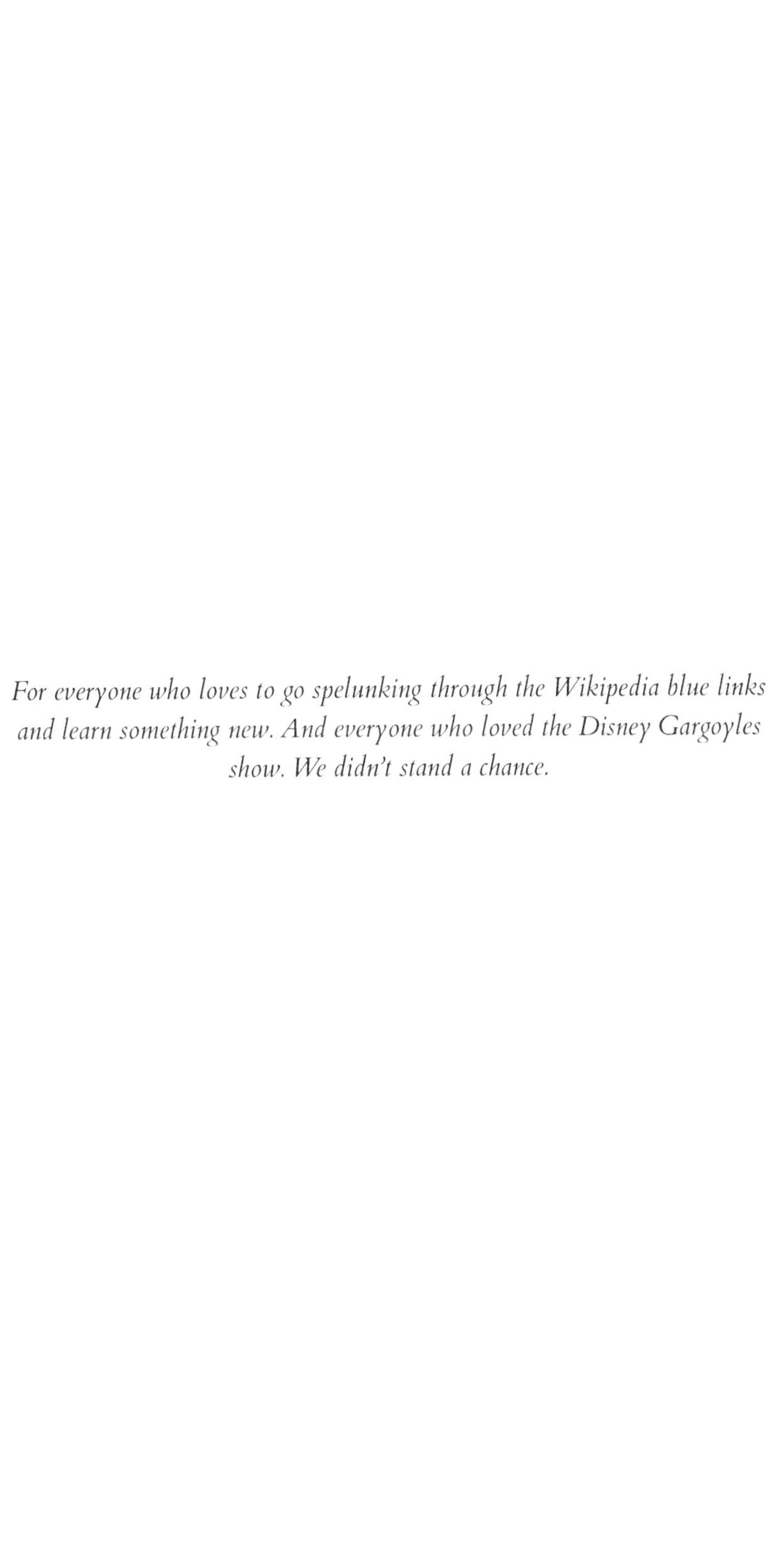

For everyone who loves to go spelunking through the Wikipedia blue links and learn something new. And everyone who loved the Disney Gargoyles show. We didn't stand a chance.

Before You Begin...

I hope you're ready for a fun romp through alternate history, full of magick, monsters, and fae! *Stone Hearts* is a prequel novella to the War of the Underhill series. The first main title is *Heartsong* (available through Avon Books). This prequel is an origins story and is *not* intended to conclude or resolve anything, but rather, start everything.

The story will follow our main couple, Carys and Gavriel, through the ages. It's snippets of their story, shown to get us to the present day, where *Heartsong* and all future books will take place. So while you can expect an HFN for Carys and Gav, please be aware that this kicks off a series. Resolution or a firm ending isn't the goal.

I hope you finish this story excited for the next. It's not required to read this before *Heartsong*, but I think you'll have an even better reading experience if you do.

So I hope you enjoy this little self-indulgent fairy tale!

All righty, let's get to it!

Prologue

In a time when time was kept through song and stone and crown, a desperate people did a desperate thing. When Caesar stepped onto the shores of Albion, five legions at his back, the Pritani, the Celts of the Isle, turned to magick to save themselves.

Their magick-weavers, the druids, called upon the magicks of Albion using a language older than man. From the earth the druids pulled great stones, carving them into mighty warriors. To give them warmth, the druids offered their own blood—and to give them life, they used ancient magick. From the stones sprang terrible creatures with wings and claws and fangs, as fearsome as the Pritani's ancient enemies, the Fomorians.

Fiercer than a pack of wolves and stronger than the bears that once roamed Albion, the guardians fought alongside the Pritani against Romans, Angles, and Saxons for six hundred years.

But the magicks that gave life to the guardians had been stolen, ripped from the earth and the fae who imbued it there so long ago,

when they were the lords of Albion.
    And the fae did not suffer thieves . . .

Part 1

One

574 AD
Western Coast of Albion

Shielding her eyes with one delicate, clawed hand, Carys peered into the sky. Her stomach swooped to behold the noonday sun. *Surely it cannot be that late!*

Shouldering her satchel, she hurried through the forest, the little path she'd worn nearly swallowed by the verdant green of springtime. She flapped her wings for more speed, batting ferns and saplings away in her excitement as she raced back to the clanhome in long bounds.

The wind swept her long sandy hair from her face, and the bright spring sun glimmered along the gold veining pattern in her skin. She'd gotten her mother's coloring, all blushing pinks and golds, the colors of the pink marble their ancestor was carved from centuries ago.

All guardians could trace themselves to one of the First, the rock-born. Heavy with muscle and towering six to seven feet tall, taller still with their arching horns and membranous wings, their colors ranged from basalt to granite to marble, and their skin was tough as hide. Her mother took great pride in their kin colors and strength, always happy to show off how the gold striations glittered off her hard warrior's body in the right light.

It was why Carys's diminutive horns, tiny claws and talons, small stature, and above all her malformed wings, shamed her mother, Arda. "How could our line come to *this?*" she'd bemoan, pointing an accusing claw at Carys. As if Carys had had any choice in the matter. As if Carys wouldn't give anything to be a female her mother could be proud of, one her clan didn't look upon with pity, one a mate could love.

She'd been trained to fight alongside the other fledglings for a time, but she was no warrior, so Carys apprenticed under the human druids in nearby Caerdyf to learn their magicks and healing. Her mother scoffed that Carys may as well have been human with her softer features and human height, but she couldn't argue with Carys making herself useful. The clan chief allowed her to travel to the human village, on the other side of the valley, several times a moon.

Carys took a little pride in her growing skills; she hoped a mate would, too—enough at least to overlook her faults.

The path grew steep, and she dug her talons into the earth to begin the climb up to the clanhome. Her clan had made a home from the natural caves burrowing into sloping seaside cliffs, perfect for flying in and out and watching over the shore and Caerdyf.

There had been a time, hundreds of years ago, when the guardians fought and lived alongside the Pritani, but as they grew in number, they'd been pushed out of the human villages and went in search of good, fertile places to make their own. Perhaps it was just as well. Her kind needed room and access to the sky; it wasn't in their nature to huddle together in small dwellings like the humans.

There were now many clans, spread across the western forests of Albion. They were protective and territorial in nature, made for fighting, and in times when there were no invaders to battle, her kin could be a volatile lot with too many horns to knock together. So the elders decided to make many settlements, but every so often, on special days, days like Beltane, *today*, the clans came together again for the Gorsedd, the great gathering.

Carys's wings shivered with excitement, and she pushed herself to go faster up the path she'd worn in the opposite slope. Her hips and thighs had grown thick and strong from the exertion, so unlike her female kin with their broad shoulders and chests, large from the work of flight. Her mother dismayed at her thick thighs and narrow shoulders, but they served Carys well as she bounded up the slope.

All guardians looked forward to the Gorsedd, a full day and night of celebration and feasting. The old stories were told over great bonfires, and new ones were invented deep into cups of mead and mulled wine. Friends chatted as clan gossip spread like pollen in springtime, thick and muzzy.

But best of all, those who hadn't yet found their heartsong, their *mate*, gathered to see if it was finally their turn.

Please let it be my turn.

Every guardian longed for that moment of *knowing* when they'd found their mate. They could love others, but only a mate stirred the heartsong, a wild, fierce song of love, recognition, belonging. And fledglings.

Though they could lay with anyone, only mates could produce offspring. Mates were never a given—for some this was a relief, like those whose heart was already claimed or who didn't love the other sex. The bestowal of matehood was as fickle as the goddesses—for some it came early in life, for others not until late, and for some not at all. It meant their people were always small in number and every fledgling born was cherished.

No one, not the rock-born nor the druids who made them, understood this quirk of their creation. The elders considered it a blessing and a curse. There was nothing stronger than a mated pair, and it would be through them that the kin lines continued. Yet that strength was kept in check, never too great to threaten the humans who first created them.

"Never enough for us to make *designs*," her father had liked to say as he and his friends commiserated over an evening cup of mead.

Fledglings were precious, even more so now that so few were being born. Neither the druids nor the elders understood that, either, but it seemed as more of their island was claimed by invaders, the fewer guardians were born.

Still, it wasn't the possibility of her own fledglings that had her racing through the clanhome.

The Gorsedd was many things to many guardians; to Carys, it was the chance, the hope of belonging. To have someone who loved and cherished her, who saw more than just her size and useless wings . . .

If fledglings came from that, well . . . all the better, she supposed.

But what will this line come to with fledglings from you? she thought in her mother's voice.

In her chamber, Carys dove into the oak trunk that held all her worldly things. There wasn't much, though with her two older sisters mated and gone, she'd come in to a few things.

Holding the ends with careful fingertips, Carys admired the abalone necklace her eldest sister had given her. The iridescent greens and blues gleamed in the slants of afternoon light sneaking in through the cracks and hollows of the cave. She fastened it around her neck, the cool shell against her skin making her shiver in delight.

Carys wanted to look her very best, hoping her future mate would quickly overlook her smallness and malformed wings. He would be strong, with wide shoulders that rippled when he flexed his wings. His claws would be long and wicked but gentle, so gentle on her. And his eyes . . . he would have kind eyes that saw everything in her she wanted to see, too.

She pulled the fine tunic that had once been her sister's over her head, careful not to snag a horn on the intricate embroidery she'd painstakingly stitched. The supple softness of the leather boots her other sister had gifted her caressed her legs as she carefully pulled them on, aligning her talons inside just so. They were her first new pair, as their mother only ever bothered to get Carys used boots the older fledglings grew out of.

To her hair she added a wooden comb, carved by her father from bleached driftwood she'd found as a child. She ran a finger over the smooth shaft, glad to carry a piece of him with her today.

Carys had attended many Gorsedds, had watched many guardians find their heartsongs, including her own sisters. She'd spent many prowling the edges of the gathering, just *waiting* to feel that pull, but by dawn nursing a goblet of mead and more disappointment.

She was five-and-twenty, a good, eligible age. Usually, Carys contented herself with the thought that if not this time, next.

But today was different. Today, she just *knew* deep down in the core of her where all her dreams and hurts and wishes lived, would be different from the rest.

Perhaps it was merely fancy, perhaps even desperation, or perhaps . . .

"Isn't that your sister's necklace?"

Carys tensed, like prey preparing to run. She hadn't heard her mother enter.

Arda already had her fists planted on her hips, her scowl thunderous.

"She gave it to me. To wear to the Gorsedd."

Arda's eyes darkened like a thundercloud.

Carys's sigh was small and quiet, the luminous excitement in her chest dimming. Arda had always been a difficult female, prone to foul moods, but had been more bearable when her sourness was spread between Carys's sisters and father.

Arda had grown pricklier since the death of Carys's father last summer. Carys dearly missed him, his steady presence and protective wing. She'd spent many afternoons huddled under her father's wings as they waited for one of Arda's rages to burn out. Her mother had howled in anguish for days when he passed, and she mourned him still, but all her grief fixed on her youngest fledgling—her smallest, different, *wrong* fledgling—and since then, Arda's anger had grown from brash to cruel.

Carys sometimes thought her parents disproved what the elders claimed about matehood. It didn't always mean love, respect, or happiness. But she had to believe her mate would love her the way her sisters' mates adored them. She had to believe that if even Arda could find a mate, so could she. But she had to believe too that it was something about Arda that made her parents' matehood a broken thing, something inherent in *her*.

Arda's lambent gaze traveled down Carys's fine tunic and soft boots. Her mouth thinned to a displeased line.

"You're not going to the Gorsedd, so take it off."

The words fell between them with all the weight and impact of a landslide. Carys's jaw dropped in shocked outrage.

"But—"

Arda's claws cut through the air, a brutal dismissal.

"No. Your sisters found their mates, the line will continue through them, thank the goddesses. But *you*," she spat, "your wings, it's a disgrace. Fewer fledglings are born every year. Those that are must be strong."

"Mother . . ." Carys choked on the venom, unready for such a malicious strike.

"I won't let you make us weaker." Arda backed slowly to the chamber entrance with the lethal calm of a coiling snake. "The line must be protected. Our strength is all we have."

Carys stood numbly, her mother's words and the mad glint in her eyes paralyzing her with fear. But it was Arda's voice, so measured, that scared Carys most.

She's gone mad—she's finally gone mad!

A horrid screech scraped her ears. With a heave, Arda pulled a monstrous boulder into the chamber entrance. Another followed, then came thick logs with their branches broken into points, sealing up the entrance.

"No!" Carys cried, falling on the barricade. "You can't do this!"

Unable to move the boulders, Carys attacked the logs, the thick bark biting back as she sliced with her claws. Splinters gouged her hands, but Carys kept clawing.

She shredded a log to pulp with her claws, freeing up a small hole. A fist slammed into Carys's face, the full force of a seasoned guardian warrior knocking her to the ground in a trembling heap of wings and limbs.

"It must end with you," Arda said, her words an ominous echo that reverberated in Carys's mind long after the entrance had been completely sealed up.

Carys remained sprawled on the ground for a long while, her swollen jaw throbbing and torn fingers stinging. Silent tears made hot tracks down her cheeks, but she was past the point of truly crying.

She came back to herself in increments, assessing each new ache and pain with a healer's detachment. Her hip smarted, her tail felt sprained where it lay under her legs, and her wings—her hideous, worthless wings!—they slumped, unable to stay upright.

With the entrance shuttered, darkness gathered in pools too thick for the errant sunbeams to penetrate. It was slow work crawling to her sleeping nest, and even slower pulling out each splinter with her teeth.

She'd lost the little light by the time she finished, and then there was nothing for Carys to do but stare at the blocked-up entrance of her chamber, its silhouette ghoulish in the deep shadows.

The tears came faster, falling from her chin in fat drops. She let them fall, cocooning herself in blankets as her breaking heart surpassed all other pains.

She didn't let herself think of the Gorsedd. She didn't think about what Arda would say, what excuses she'd make—

It must end with you.

Carys jerked upright, fighting back panic.

What if she doesn't let me out even after the Gorsedd?

Frantic, Carys leapt to her shaky feet to probe the rockfall, hunting for weaknesses. Branches snapped under her claws, but the barricade held.

Her panic sharpening into cold desperation, Carys paced the chamber and considered something she very much didn't want to do, something she hadn't done since she was a fledgling.

It cannot be worse than dying here in the dark.

No, it couldn't be.

Feeling along the wall, Carys found the little nook, her little secret. In the far wall, a narrow crevice opened in the rock.

Wrapping her wings around her middle, Carys wedged herself into the tight opening. The rocks scraped her, but she made herself fit. Inside, the crevice jutted upward, following a thick tree root to the forest and sky above.

Carys clambered up, stealing breaths where it was wide enough for her chest to expand. Her fingers howled in pain, and more than one claw broke on the unyielding rock, sending a burst of sparks to the ground below.

She stopped twice, exhausted, wedged between the rockfaces, and considered going back.

But then she growled at herself. She wouldn't meet her mate today, but goddesses help her, she *would not* die today, either.

She kept going, determined now if only to defy Arda. The smell of crisp air spurred her on, and when she spied the pinks and purples of a dusky sky, Carys threw herself at the opening. Squirming through, she ignored her cramping wings and trembling legs. She collapsed on the grassy clifftop and drank down the cool evening air in gulps.

The clouds spun above her as her pulse throbbed at her temples.

Carys couldn't help the laugh that bubbled up, a defiant thing that beckoned a roar after it that carried across the sea. Carys screamed until her voice was as raw as her hands. She thought of all those curses the druids knew, the ones born of forbidden magicks, and wished all of them on Arda.

She staggered to standing and spat on the clifftop, done with this place and her mother.

Her eldest sister had invited her to stay with her in her mate's clan. Carys would go there. She'd build something new for herself, mate or no.

But there was one thing she must do first.

Turning her aching body downhill, Carys made not for the Gorsedd but the place she was happiest.

The old well.

Two

Gavriel had almost forgotten about the rifts, where the borders of the Underhill were just weak enough for someone to peer through to the other realms. Someone like him.

Deep in the Underhill, Gavriel had found a rift entirely by accident in his wanderings. It was small, merely an old well in the mortal realm of Albion. Rifts always required water, something to do with its life-giving nature or perhaps its ability to carry magick further than air or if not that then simply its power to erode. Gavriel couldn't remember. Just another memory lost to the endless gloam of the Underhill. Memories, borders, rifts, all were easily lost in the nebulous darkness, always shifting like smoke in the wind.

Gavriel came across a flash of blue sky one day, something he hadn't seen in almost a thousand years—and would've missed it were it not for the spot of pink at its center, like roses blushing into bloom. He'd been drawn to the brilliant colors, to *her*, like a moth to the flame.

The view from the rift was distorted, like looking through water, but he saw a pink female face peering down at him, her wide yellow eyes framed in thick lashes. It was only when her mouth formed a perfect o of surprise, a sight that *did something* to him, that Gavriel realized she could see him, too.

It'd shocked her almost as much as it did him.

She sparked something inside him, sensations old and new, and in the end, he couldn't resist the temptation of her. Every day he returned to the rift, and every day he found her there waiting for him. They discovered they could hear each other, even if the sound warbled, as though it traveled down a long, damp tunnel.

They spoke often, wiling away afternoons. He told her old tales of the goddesses and the seven realms. She described the landscape outside the well for him, the vast stretches of rolling hills, the blankets of rich grasses and wildflowers. She was generous and patient, describing the texture of flower petals and the color of storms. His lonely heart soaked up her words and kindness, beginning to live for when he slipped away from the fae court to see his odd pink maiden.

They did not speak of their lives nor exchange names. Neither offered nor asked. For Gavriel, he feared if he did, if he pushed for more than he'd already been given, it would all disappear, snatched away as surely as sunlight and fresh air had been when he and all the fae bound themselves to the Underhill.

Why the female didn't ask, he didn't know. He didn't care, either. What mattered was that she returned to him, day after day, offering him respite from the cold fate he and his kin had resigned themselves to, if only for a while.

In another life, Gavriel had been one of the Faerie Queen's generals. He'd fought beside Queen Rhiannon, Lady Morrígan, and his brothers-in-arms for many mortal years to stem the Fomorian incursion, a battle his forebears had waged against the vicious creatures from another realm many times and won.

Gavriel and his brothers had not.

The Fomorians had seen how the fae, blessed by the goddesses, could move between their realm of Faerie and the mortal realm of Albion and grew covetous. They broke free of their dark, watery realm into Albion, determined to conquer and consume all in their path. Wave after wave, century after century, the fae had met and beaten back the incursion in Albion, the only thing between Faerie and an insatiable horde that devoured magick and flesh.

A thousand years ago, the fae, children of the goddess Danu, lost everything to those beasts.

It was cruel that of all the memories lost to the murky gloom of the Underhill, he still remembered every detail of that last battle. He remembered retreating from Albion and how the barricades fell behind them, a writhing mass of Fomorians swarming the borders of Faerie itself; he could still feel the dark blood splattered across his face, still hear the clang of fae steel meeting horn and hide.

Gavriel could easily lose himself in those memories, slip into that dark pit of shame for failing his kin and queen. Faerie had lasted only a few days more, the creatures eating the very magick that made up the realm's protections. Gorged on the barrier itself, the Fomorians swept through Faerie like a wildfire, leaving nothing behind but smoke and ash.

Faerie couldn't be saved, and the fae were forced to take their only chance—fleeing through the sídhe, the ancient gateways between realms. They sought shelter in the Underhill, the realm under all the others, one of caves, warrens, and roots. Though every realm kept its own borders, they were tied together by ancient tendrils far older than the fae. Before the Fomorians invaded, only the fae had been able to traverse these tethers between realms. They couldn't be broken, even by someone as strong as Rhiannon, but they could be blocked.

To prevent the Fomorians from pursuing them into the Underhill, Rhiannon summoned all the power of their people as only a Faerie

Queen could. Alongside her sister Morrígan, her duality and balance, Rhiannon stoppered every opening and shored up every border of the Underhill. But even for Rhiannon, magick had its price.

Morrígan was lost to the spell. Their magick, a gift given long ago by Danu, was stripped away from their very beings, used to fortify the borders between realms. Bound up in her spell, every living fae became tethered to the Underhill. The Fomorians were locked out of the Underhill, and the fae inside.

The irony of the following centuries sat bitter on his tongue.

For many dark decades, the Fomorians ravaged Faerie and Albion, glutting on all the remaining creatures and magicks. But they hadn't reigned for long. In longboats from the south, humans arrived on Albion to fight the Fomorians, now fat and lazy from their feast. The humans should have been nothing against those beasts, with their fangs, wings, and claws, but through sheer numbers, stubbornness, and having no innate magick for the Fomorians to feed upon, the humans slaughtered every creature and closed the rip between realms.

All this the fae watched from inside the boundless confines of the Underhill. Gavriel spent countless years driving himself to insanity trying to make sense of it, how the Fomorians had been able to break through borders that had stood for eons, how humans had been able to do what the fae hadn't, what *Gavriel* hadn't. He tormented himself with these questions until, finally, he buried them and his rage and everything else he'd once been deep inside, in the cavity where his magick had once lived. There was nothing else to be done.

The Fomorians were gone, but Faerie was all but destroyed and humans now claimed Albion. All that was left to the fae was the Underhill, a realm that did not want them but were now bound to. It was the fate they had chosen. For a thousand years, that resignation and his own failure had been Gavriel's companions as he and his kin withered in the darkness.

Until one day, an odd, beautiful pink face peered down at him through the gloom.

He didn't know how long he'd been meeting his mysterious maiden, as he'd lost most sense of time. It passed and stood still all at once for the fae, long-lived as they were.

However long it was, Gavriel could sense when she approached the rift, feeling something like a caress running down his spine, a lover's touch. Perhaps it should have unnerved him, but in the lonely boredom of his existence, Gavriel breathed a sigh of pleasure whenever that delicious shiver ran down his back. *She's close.*

He quickened his pace, abandoning the usual circuit he made of the known borders. His path to the rift was shorter every day. That was the way of the Underhill; well-worn paths remained and drew closer together, while forgotten routes were reclaimed by the darkness.

It seemed to only take a few steps and then there it was, a halo of lavender in the gloom. Climbing a fall of rubble and dirt to get closer, Gavriel's boots found the packed indentations of his many hours standing in this exact spot.

His blood rushed hot at the sight of golden hair fluttering in an evening breeze.

"Good day, female," he called. Then winced.

Perhaps once he might've thought of something charming to say, though Rhiannon often teased him for being dour, but whatever small charm he'd once had drained away in the years underground.

His grumbling pride was nothing, though, compared to the pleasure of beholding her lovely face, limned in the roses and lilacs of dusk.

She smiled down at him, the first stars sparkling around her head like a crown, and Gavriel felt lit from within by her radiance.

"You came," she said, a breathiness to her voice that had him digging his boots further into the dirt.

"I'm yours to command," he replied, trying for levity, knowing it was more like truth.

"You weren't here and I thought . . ." She shook her head. "You've said before you can go . . . elsewhere."

Gavriel's lips parted, to say what he didn't know. How strange her words were; they stirred a thread of unease in him.

"I don't mind. I would wait . . ." *forever.*

There were worse ways to spend eternity than waiting for every spare moment of his pink maiden's company, but Gavriel knew it was far more than that, more than the loneliness that dogged his soul.

It was something deep, deeper even than blood or bone or viscera. It lived in the very core of him, filling up a hollow center where magick had once flowed, magick that had made his people some of the most powerful in the seven realms. He'd felt the lack of his magick for centuries like a lost limb, a chasm left inside him by the constant siphon of the Underhill's tether. But when Gavriel beheld her, he swore something sparked in his chest, tugging against its tether.

"I'm glad you don't have to haunt this well waiting for me."

"I was . . ."

His words trailed away as he searched her face. Between the filmy barrier and the shadow of the well, he never saw her clearly, and in the fading light, he thought perhaps the purpling along her left cheek and jaw was merely shadow.

No. The light was wrong for that, the color was wrong.

Bruises. Someone had struck her, hard enough to leave proof.

Something inside him snapped, releasing a sharp, consuming fury the likes of which he hadn't felt since he last gutted a Fomorian.

"Sweetling . . ." The endearment fell from his lips without thought or regret. "Who did this to you?"

Her face broke in a sob.

The dark fury in him howled—for her pain, for retribution, for freedom. He needed *out*, to comfort her, to destroy whatever did this. Power crackled through him, sizzling in his veins, a strength he hadn't felt in centuries.

He placed his palm on the cool face of the barrier. It thrummed under his hand—but held.

It was only by the barest thread of sanity he didn't throw himself at the barricade. A snarl rumbled in his throat, and it was through force of will he kept himself from pacing like a caged animal.

She didn't need his snarling frustration.

"What's happened, sweetling? Please tell me."

With a shudder, she reined back her tears behind a brave mask. He didn't miss how her lower lip trembled, though.

"It isn't important," she said.

"It *is* important," he implored. *It's everything.*

But she only smiled sadly. "She has no power over me anymore."

"Your mother." He couldn't help the growl.

She gave the smallest nod.

Gavriel could've cracked stone with how hard he ground his teeth. *Her mother.* She never said as much in as many words, but the torment inflicted on her, this gentle, beautiful creature, by her own mother was palpable even a realm away. He didn't know everything, had had to make many assumptions to fill in the gaps, but he knew enough to hate her mother with a depth only the Fomorians had inspired.

"I'm leaving my mother's house," she admitted, almost so quietly he didn't hear.

That unease from before, drowned out by his rage at seeing her hurt, slithered through him again.

"Leaving," he repeated, the word like ash in his mouth. "Where?"

"To my sister. But it's . . . two days' journey there. I don't think I'll be able to return. Not for a while, at least."

"You came to say goodbye."

"Yes."

If a chasm had opened beneath him to the center of the Fomorians' watery realm, it wouldn't have been half so terrifying as her words. Their promise of dark, endless wandering below the dirt and roots, waiting in abject loneliness for the Otherworld to call his soul home, tore what was left of his heart in two.

Regret nearly choked him. He'd spent months in her company, but they'd both maintained a distance, made of silences and ambiguity and, worst of all, self-created. She'd given him so much of her time, so many of her words.

Yet I don't even know her name.

"Will you be safe there?" he asked through numb lips.

She assured him she would, her sister would look after her, that this was a new beginning, a—

"Lord Gavren."

Gavriel spun toward the sound of his given name, blocking the rift with his body. He snarled at the figure materializing from the gloom, that roaring beast inside him outraged by an intruder.

The willowy form of Tiernan stopped a respectful distance away, his hands folded behind him.

Gavriel endeavored to swallow his fury. Tiernan was a good lad, barely old enough to remember a time before the Underhill. Unlike the many who let themselves forget the old ways to numb their grief, Tiernan wanted to be a true fae warrior. It was his dedication that earned him a place as squire to one of Gavriel's oldest friends, Allarand.

"What is it?" he clipped.

"I'm sorry to disturb you, but you're needed in the throne room."

Gavriel's lip curled in disgust. "What does Titania want now?"

"Not her." Tiernan's face went tight. "It's Lord Allarand. He's found something wrong with the magick."

"And he's confronting her with it?"

Tiernan grimaced.

Huffing a curse, Gavriel bit back his annoyance. His old friend was a mighty warrior with a noble heart, but goddess, he still hadn't learned to hold his tongue nor to pick his fights.

"I'll be there in a moment."

The young fae knew when he was dismissed. Bowing, he quickly disappeared into the darkness.

Gavriel sighed, chest aching as he stepped back to the rift and saw his pink maiden, head pillowed on her folded arms.

"I've been called away," he said softly, not wanting to wake her if she slept.

He was grateful when her head immediately lifted to look for him below.

"Oh," she breathed, so many things contained in one sound.

His heart beat a thready, panicked rhythm. He didn't want to leave like this. He didn't want *her* to leave like this.

"Will you wait for me?" he asked without thinking. "I'll return to you as soon as I can."

She thought for a moment, her lips parted slightly. The sight of her lips always incited wicked things in him, dark desires richer than wine and softer than velvet. He focused on those lips, willing them to say—

"Yes, I'll stay awhile."

"You won't . . . go back?"

"Never," she said with a viciousness that called to that dark thing inside him.

"Never," he agreed. He placed his palm on the barrier again, leaning as close to it as he could, hoping she could see his face clearer for it and the promise burning there. "I will return to you."

A soft smile touched her lips. "I know you will."

Gavriel felt that smile everywhere and carried it with him back into the darkness. He'd make this quick and return to her—he wasn't ready for her goodbyes.

Three

The throne room shone like an aurora, the light from every sconce captured in sparkling relief inside the amethyst-encrusted walls. In their plentiful time in the Underhill, the fae had cut, shaped, and polished the crystals until the translucent purple surfaces threw back the light in a diffused glow. The crystalline cavern was unspeakably beautiful, an unfathomable treasure, but had lost its appeal to Gavriel long ago.

The cavern seemed almost cramped today with the morbidly curious crowding in to hear Allarand's news. Tiernan had apprised him on the way, and Gavriel couldn't say he was surprised.

Perhaps it's better that she's to leave. The rift could close anytime and she'd always wonder what happened.

Fae skittered out of his way as he strode toward the throne, Tiernan trotting behind.

"Lord Gavren," they whispered respectfully, their eyes searching.

He hated that they looked but hated more that there was nothing to find. He'd stopped looking back and giving them the chance to see that he had nothing to give. He hadn't saved them when Faerie fell, and he couldn't save them now.

The throne had been given a wide berth, leaving only Allarand. He stood with feet planted wide and hands folded behind his back, a pose Gavriel had seen many times as they surveyed battlefields.

On the throne sat Titania, a delicate smirk adorning her blood-red lips. Against the glowing purple crystal, she looked like a shadow, all black and crimson brocade. Kohl lined her eyes, emphasizing their startling red hue. Her blue-black hair fell to her hips in cascading waves, diamond pins winking like stars through the tresses.

She was the daughter of Morrígan the Crow. Niece of Queen Rhiannon the Gold.

No one had seen Morrígan since the Underhill was sealed, and without her sister and her magick so devoted to the spell, Rhiannon had begun to wither away.

It'd been . . . too long since Gavriel last saw Rhiannon, but the sight of her laying in her bower unnerved him. Her faithful handmaids guarded her as she slept the eternal sleep, not quite in the Otherworld and not wholly in the Underhill either. Rhiannon couldn't truly slip away to the Otherworld, the realm of the dead, not when so much of her was tethered to the Underhill and the spell, but neither could she survive in it. The Underhill rebelled against so much power not of itself.

So Rhiannon took to the eternal sleep, enough to keep the protections in place but her power muted to placate the Underhill. It was an existence Gavriel wished on no one.

In Rhiannon's stead, Titania ruled. But still uncrowned, and her aunt still living, Titania could never harness the true power of the Faerie Queen.

Thank the goddesses.

Titania was not and would never be Gavriel's queen.

Titania made it clear over the centuries that she didn't care what

Gavriel, Allarand, or anyone else felt. She had royal blood, the purest, most powerful line left of the fae. She wasn't crowned, but Titania was more powerful than all of them, still able to wield some of her own magick. So she sat on her crystal throne, ringed by a loyal cadre of simpering courtiers, and played at being Faerie Queen.

Gavriel had made the mistake of seeing her youth and assuming she meant or could cause little harm; in her first years, the regency had worked well enough, but as Rhiannon's sleep continued and the Underhill slowly closed in around them, Titania's true nature had surfaced.

Titania's glittering ruby eyes darted to him as he approached the throne, the smirk widening to a little grin that turned Gavriel's stomach.

"Good of you to join us, Lord Gavren," said Titania, cutting across Allarand's argument.

His friend turned to him, face grave. He nodded to Gavriel, who returned it as he stopped alongside Allarand, shoulder to shoulder.

Titania looked between them. "My my, the queen's generals, coming to me so serious. Such attentions could be much better spent, my lords." She smiled wickedly, running her tongue along her full bottom lip.

Gavriel worked to keep his expression neutral, hiding his disgust. It was well known how voraciously Titania went through lovers. He didn't begrudge anyone the distraction of pleasure, and trapped as they were, no hope for anyone who hadn't already of finding truemates, *cariad*, many took comfort where they could. But Titania found pleasure not in another's touch but in the domination of them.

No, Titania's tactics wouldn't work with him. Let her use her body to reward loyalty to the cackling young warriors who ringed the throne.

Gavriel had seen warriors react in a myriad of ways to the pressures of battle. Some couldn't cope, some tore out their hair and wailed themselves sick, while others took the cruelty with them and made the world their battlefield. Some lost all sense, numb to the value of life, and lived as fast-burning flames, consuming every pleasure to be had until their time was up.

He saw all these and more gathered around the regent, whispering in her ear, eager to do her bidding.

If it was just an occasional show of power against him and Allarand, he could've borne it. For Rhiannon. But the centuries showed their toll in Titania's quick temper and paranoia.

He saw it now, a shadow of frustration just below her eye as Allarand made his argument again, voice booming, "I've been testing it myself and can find no other explanation. The Underhill is shrinking. Paths are closing up."

"The Underhill takes back what isn't used," Titania dismissed.

"We've lost more people to the dark, paths closed up behind them."

"They should know better than to wander."

A growl built in Allarand's chest, and Gavriel clasped his friend's shoulder.

"It isn't a matter of getting lost in the dark, Highness," Gavriel said.

Her smile was sharp when she turned it on Gavriel. "Lord Allarand wants me to battle the Underhill, use up my magick to reclaim some lost paths. Why, I wonder? To weaken me?"

"To rescue our people!" exclaimed Allarand.

"And how do you know they didn't just give themselves to the Otherworld?"

Disquiet hummed through the court. It was a tasteless question; the fae lost most recently were a family, one of the few mated pairs to find each other after Faerie was lost, and their child. Fae children hadn't been uncommon in Faerie, but they usually only blessed mates, *cariad*. Perhaps it was due to their natural longevity or a trait passed down by their divine ancestors. But after being trapped, matings nearly ceased and children became rare.

Titania's brow ticked. She felt it too, the quiet outrage at the insinuation.

Titania affected large, concerned eyes. "My beloved aunt, our queen, sacrifices everything to keep us safe. She appointed me as regent while she pits her will against the Underhill. Our family sacrifices our power every day for our people. And now you would ask me to put them in danger just to reclaim a few walking paths?"

"He's asking you to protect your people," Gavriel said. "If your magick cannot repel it, cannot keep us safe, then other plans must be made."

Those plush lips disappeared into her mouth and her ruby eyes burned hotter than hellfire, but she knew her answer could turn the court against her.

She sat in simmering silence, glaring between Gavriel and Allarand, but both were too experienced to cower at the frown of a monarch. Titania's glower was nothing to the snapping jaws of a Fomorian—or even the scowl of her mother, Morrígan.

No, he wasn't afraid of her frown—it was her sudden, loud laugh that chilled his blood.

"You make a point, Lord Gavren," she cooed. "My power isn't great enough to do what Lord Allarand asks. But we can remedy that."

She arched a perfect brow, reveling in the bated silence. Gavriel clenched his fists behind his back.

"We can never be fully protected from the Underhill because we don't have all our magick. The humans stole magick to make their creatures." Titania stood, casting her voice to fill the cavern. "I will reclaim what was stolen and use that power to fight back the Underhill. I call for a Hunt!"

Dread lanced through Gavriel. A Hunt. A punch of power to break into the mortal realm. It was dangerous, reckless, and required a considerable burst of magick. But the reward . . .

It'd been centuries ago, the memory hazy like so many others, but all fae felt it when the magick imbued within Albion long ago was taken. Rhiannon had rushed to soothe the wounds, but he knew cost her.

The fae muttered at the suggestion, and Gavriel realized a moment after Titania, a moment too late, that the court was amenable.

Her smile was all teeth as she declared, "Tonight is Beltane, the rifts shall be thin. We ride at midnight to reclaim what's ours!"

The court cheered, exploding into activity.

Titania turned to Gavriel and Allarand, all triumph and glittering ruby eyes. "You will accompany us, my lords, to ensure our success. It's for our people, after all."

Titania descended the throne and lost herself in the flock of courtiers, declaring loudly to prepare mounts.

Allarand's face went ashen. "I didn't mean—"

"She'll need all our power to get through," Gavriel said. "Delay as long as you can." And then he was pushing through the crowd, desperate to get to *her*.

Their creatures . . .

How could he have missed it? The human and Fomorian features . . . how could he not have seen his maiden was one of those magickborn creatures?

He had to warn her.

"Where are you going?" Allarand called after him.

But he didn't waste time answering. Gavriel disappeared into the gloom, running faster than when Faerie had fallen around him.

Four

Carys made herself comfortable on a bed of ferns and brush. She might've laughed at herself, waiting on a ghost she talked to through a well, but tonight, her broken heart wanted a friendly face. She'd come to say goodbye, yes, but didn't mind delaying a little.

She didn't want to say goodbye at all.

She'd stumbled upon the well one day foraging, and while lowering her cup for water, a face had appeared, haunting, beautiful, and just as surprised to see her. Her lonely heart hadn't been able to resist returning to him, day after day.

His face may have been murky, his voice a watery echo, but everything about him was dear. He listened for hours to her talk of nothing. They spent afternoons reciting ballads and terrible jokes. They played word games and made fantastical shapes from the clouds—his were always terrible.

Sometimes she spoke of her life, though she never admitted much. Perhaps it was cowardly, but he never spoke of his, either. Not who he'd been or what had trapped him in the well. There were times when his face was clear enough that she thought she spied ears pointed like hers and eyes that flashed quicksilver. The druids spoke of beings who had inhabited Albion before them, ethereal creatures who fought and died against the demons that had ruled the island when the Pritani themselves arrived. Perhaps he was one of those unfortunate beings, resigned to where he'd been slain.

There was something terribly tragic yet romantic about it. But Carys knew her friend's fate must have been a painful one, and tragedies were rarely romantic for those who lived them.

She wanted to know everything about her ghost, but she wouldn't ask if it might pain him. She'd hoped that maybe, one day, he'd trust her with his story.

But she was leaving.

And she didn't even know his name.

Carys blew out a breath, saddened all over again. All the emotions of the day had drained away, leaving her with only the stings of her many small wounds. She'd have to wait until morning to see to them, so she closed her eyes and breathed in the spring night, trying to—

"*You must run!*"

Carys sprang to her feet, looking around wildly for a threat but found nothing, the night dark and still.

She hurried to the well. The night was bright by the full moon and glittering stars, but the well still looked like a bottomless chasm straight to the underworld.

A frantic face broke up the darkness, quicksilver eyes flashing in the shadows.

"You're here," he gasped in relief.

"I promised I'd wait."

He nodded, but rather than looking pleased, his mouth thinned into a grim line. Carys's stomach clenched; she wouldn't like his next words.

"You must go—run and don't look back."

"I told you I'm going to my sister's."

"No," he growled, "take your sister and run. They're coming for you, for the magick that was stolen."

Cold terror struck Carys's chest. *Magick stolen.* The druids rarely dabbled in true magick anymore, their powers and connection to Albion weakened by the constant invasions and infighting. What magick was left resided in the guardians, Carys's people.

All younglings were told the legends of how the First had been shaped from rock, given warmth by human blood, but granted life with magick taken from Albion, magick imbued by those ethereal beings, the fae, long ago.

Fae. A shiver skittered down her spine. Younglings were warned about the wrath of the fae, how they tricked mortals into the underworld, switched newborns with their own changelings, and haunted crossroads—looking for their stolen magick.

The fae were coming to reclaim what was stolen.

"But how . . .?"

"The veil is thin on Beltane. Please, sweetling, don't let them find you!" he demanded, face larger and brighter, as if he pressed against whatever kept him inside the well.

Shocked still in her terror, Carys stared at that terrible, terrified, ethereal face. Tonight he seemed clearer than before, like a reflection on still water rather than rippling fractals.

Silver eyes shone in a strong face, set below slashing black brows and above a sharp nose with flaring nostrils. Cheekbones like carved marble curved toward ears long and pointed that kept back a waterfall of hair the color of starlight. His skin shone opalescent, not quite white or gray or tanned, gleaming with pinks and greens.

He was painfully beautiful in his fury, and it made the churning unease in Carys's belly harden.

"How do you know this?" she asked through numb lips.

His brow ticked and he shook his head. "There isn't time, I'm called away. But I—please, *fy annwyl*, run and never come back. *Go!*"

His voice reverberated up the well, hitting her like a physical blow. Carys staggered back, limbs shaking.

Her fear kept her rooted beside the well, the hoot of an owl sending her jumping.

The night was soft around her, twinkling stars in a velvet sky and the titters and coos of nocturnal animals. Too calm and quiet for her ghost's ill tidings.

If what he said was true, there wasn't much time. She didn't know where she could hide from the fae themselves, how anything could stop beings so powerful, but she—

She had to warn them.

The Gorsedd. Beltane. Everyone, all her kin, gathered in one place. "Goddesses save us."

She made her feet move, one then the other, until she was running blindly through the forest. It was at least an hour by wing to the Gorsedd glen, but Carys could only run. And she did, she ran, as fast as she could, flapping her wings to extend her bounds.

Her wings may have been malformed, but that night, Carys flew.

Five

Gavriel flew through the darkness, his mount surging beneath him, surrounded on all sides by dozens of eager fae. Sparks sizzled from the nostrils of their mounts, ancient scaly creatures they'd long ridden but never quite tamed, with long muzzles full of dagger teeth and capable of spitting fire.

Titania rode at the front atop the alpha female. She'd clad herself in dark red leathers, a mimicry of the traditional fae armor Gavriel and Allarand wore. Light but strong, the leather and metal moved with him, and strapping it on had felt like greeting an old friend. But now, amongst a pack of bloodthirsty fae, the armor felt like vestiges of a male who no longer existed, a costume just as much as Titania's concoction.

Round a bend and then there was the sídhe, pulsing an otherworldly gold. Outside lay Albion, the Green Isle. Unlike the rifts, mere weak points in the Underhill, the sídhes were gateways between realms and where most of the magick barricading them inside concentrated. Nothing got through without a massive thrust of power, the likes of which only a royal fae could command.

Titania put on speed. Wisps of magick gathered around her, coalescing in a ball of light brighter than the sun itself. When Titania hurled it against the gate, the veil trembled before a hole melted in its center, globs of molten magick falling away.

Titania bound through the hole, leading the Hunt into the mortal realm for the first time in centuries.

Gavriel braced himself as his mount leapt into the night. Fresh air caressed his skin, and tears gathered in his eyes at the smell of green and the sound of the wind.

For one glorious moment, they were free.

But the further they went, the tauter their tethers to the Underhill drew and the stronger the pull to return became. It began in Gavriel's gut, a twisting discomfort, before setting his teeth on edge. Their tethers to the Underhill would only allow them to go so far for so long, even with Titania's power.

They wouldn't have long.

They raced through the forest, closing in on a warm glow emanating through the trees. The sounds of celebration and smells of roasting spits and flowing ale overcame his fine fae senses, the memories of such good things tugging at him harder than the Underhill.

The Hunt burst from the trees, shadows with teeth and steel.

Screams pulled him from his reverie.

Gavriel jerked on the reins, Allarand and Tiernan stopping alongside him. The mounts stomped, wanting to follow the pack, but Gavriel kept a firm hold on his.

He wouldn't take part in this carnage.

The druid-made creatures had held their celebration in a glen, bonfires scattered around a main fire where meals cooked and people congregated. Titania led a vanguard straight for that heart of the gathering. She and her favorites, pampered youths who didn't remember the Fomorian Wars, who played at being warriors for their amusement, slashed their way through, cut down any who tried to stop them.

Screams rent the air, and some of the creatures leapt into the sky, taking their young, only to plummet again with arrows in their backs. Fae mounts sprang to catch others, bringing them down with ripped wings and limbs.

She's safe, I warned her, she isn't here . . .

"Lord Allarand . . ." Tiernan murmured, eyes wide with horror.

Allarand laid a heavy hand on his shoulder, steadying him. It was all they could do.

Is this what we've become, lost in the dark so long?

This wasn't reclaiming the magick. This was slaughter, bloodlust born of boredom and cruelty. He tried not to hear the screams or the wet sounds of metal and fangs sinking into flesh.

If this was what the fae had been reduced to, slavering feral beasts, then they deserved to rot in the dark until the Otherworld took them.

"They're fighting back," Allarand observed.

She's safe, she isn't here . . .

Gavriel's gaze strayed back to the melee, unable to stop from searching for her pink face.

He didn't know what he'd do if he found it.

With the ambush revealed, dozens of warriors used their bodies to rebuff the Hunt from the center fire, giving others time to flee or rescue the wounded. They flashed their wings and claws, dragging down fae that strayed too close.

From one moment to the next, the battle shifted. Titania and her favorites, faced with seasoned fighters, were beaten back.

Even from the trees, Gavriel saw when Titania lost her patience. With an impatient wave of her clawed hand, her favorites rallied around to protect her as she summoned her magick. An eerie glow limned Titania's frame, magick sparking from her palms. Her lips twitched with the effort, and the force of calling so much magick whipped her black hair about her face as if she stood inside a tempest. The eye of the storm.

One by one, colorful threads unspooled from the creatures, limning them too in light. They slithered to the ground but wouldn't stray far from the creatures, who groaned and shuddered as the magick tried to resist but was compelled out.

For long moments Titania called, but the magick refused to come to her.

"Something's wrong," Gavriel murmured. "She can't—"

Suddenly, the wisps snuffed like a candle, and even from his place in the trees, Gavriel marked the vicious frown creasing Titania's face.

Standing in her saddle, Titania cried, "*Magick stolen and rent away, forsake these thieves to blood and stone; untether from this mortal realm, return now to the Faerie throne!*"

Magick as pure and hot as lightning sizzled across the glen. The creatures howled and writhed, the magick that gave them life bursting out like blood from a wound, gushing and devastating. Their limbs went stiff, their faces frozen in terror. Those that were airborne fell and shattered.

It took only one horrible moment, and then it was over, the magick sucked away, leaving only stone husks.

The glen went quiet, a necropolis of statues, save for the buzzing crackle of the magick radiating from Titania. Her hair whipped about her head wildly, and her eyes glowed a pure blue, iris and pupil consumed.

When she smiled, it was a horrible thing.

"And now," she said in a terrible, deep voice, "for those that made them."

With a savage cry, she led the Hunt northward, their bloodlust hungering for the druids who'd stolen the magick in the first place.

Gavriel, Allarand, and Tiernan lingered in the trees.

"Goddess have mercy on them," Allarand breathed.

Mercy wouldn't show her face tonight, too horrified at what had already been done.

Gavriel swallowed on a dry throat, the ache in his chest greater even than the pull of the Underhill.

She's safe, I warned her. She's . . .

He couldn't spend the rest of his dark days wondering.

He dismounted, and the fae mount huffed and slithered away to join its pack.

His boots squelched in the bloody mud, the tang of blood, offal, and terror overwhelming his senses as he descended into the glen.

"Gavren!" Allarand called after him.

But Gavriel went. He needed to know.

It was nearly dawn when Carys careened into the Gorsedd glen. Her lungs and limbs burned from exertion, and her fangs clacked together as she heaved for breath.

She wiped away sweat that dripped into her eyes. Then blinked, wondering if it was the meager light that made all the guardians so pallid. The fires had burned down to coals. Bodies lay or stood or crouched, unmoving, unnatural.

But . . . why didn't they move?

Uneasiness gripped her innards. She trembled as she crept into the quiet glen.

Carys rounded the first guardian she found, a big male with his arm extended. She made to ask what had happened, had the fae already come, but what left her mouth was a gasp of horror.

Frozen in a rictus of fear, the male's eyes were empty stone. Carys touched him with a shaky hand only to snatch it back, his arm cold and smooth.

He was . . . he was . . .

Her chest clenched in dread as she crept further into the glen.

But she already knew what she'd find.

Males, females, fledglings, elders—they'd all turned to stone. She stumbled through the stone corpses, lifeless and still and their faces petrified.

She found true corpses closer to the central fire, the smell of eviscerated flesh making her gag. She stopped at the sight of the slaughter, unable to go closer.

There'd been a battle here, a fight for their very existence. And they'd lost.

Carys stumbled back from the massacre, searching the stone faces instead. She didn't know, or didn't want to know, what she searched for until she found it.

Her eldest sister crouched, one hand wrapped around an arrow jutting from her thigh and the other clutching her mate, who held her up with his wings spread over them as a shield. The granite of his hand blended seamlessly with her pink marble shoulder.

Nearby, her other sister lay dead, throat ripped out as if she'd been set upon by beasts. Her mate lay beside her, his chest crushed. Their mother was a few steps away, eyes wide but unseeing, one of her wings rent from its socket.

Her breaths came quick but shallow, none reaching her lungs. Carys clutched at her chest, sure it was caving in. The world spun, and she lurched away, bile burning her throat.

Carys fell to her knees and howled. She clutched her arms around herself, as if she could hold herself together when everything else had fallen apart. How could this have happened? How could anything fell a warrior like her mother or sisters?

I should have been here.

The anger at being locked away and left behind still burned bright in her chest, and she hated herself for it. She hated that it'd saved her, and she hated that she hadn't perished with her kin.

Her loud, gasping tears were sure to draw every predator for miles. *Good. Let them come.* Let the fae finish what they'd begun. She might be small, but she'd fight, claw, bite, and meet her ancestors, her kin, with pride. She'd take as many as she—

Something moved in the corner of her eye, blurry through her tears. Her head whipped to the right, hope and fear knotting her throat.

For a moment, she saw nothing but empty stone faces. Then one of them blinked.

Carys hissed and leapt up.

A gray figure loomed over the charred remains of a bonfire. No, not gray, opalescent, gleaming with greens and pinks in the growing daylight. Deep-set eyes the color of mercury stared at her in a painfully handsome face.

She knew that face.

Something tugged at her chest, hard and insistent, as if her heart had been roped and pulled. She felt it down to her talons and wingtips, a tingling flush of *knowing*.

It was *him*, her ghost. Staring at her, alive and breathing and and—

Fae.

He was *fae*.

That's how he knew to warn her. He'd known his people came to annihilate hers. And he'd helped. Of course he had, standing there in armor with blood on his boots.

His tall frame rocked forward, as though he felt a pull too, and Carys hissed again.

He blinked at the sound, as if coming awake, and his perfect lips formed a single word.

"*Cariad*."

Her name but not. The strange sound set her heart racing, urges and sensations pulsing through her that couldn't be true, not *here*, not with *him*.

She shook her head. It was his magick affecting her, trying to draw her in. *It had to be.*

His mouth thinned to a firm line and then he was moving, all graceful predator as he stalked around the firepit.

Her heart seized, the pull tugging her toward him, her anguish goading her to attack and be done with it.

But instead Carys ran—from him, from the glen and the tragedy there, ran and ran and ran. Like the coward she was.

Seven

Gavriel gave chase. A primal urgency drove him, the thrill of pursuit and instinct to hunt intoxicating. He'd never felt it with such intensity, this burning need to pursue, capture, and claim.

Because it was her. *Cariad.* Staring at him across the wreckage of her people.

Goddesses, how had he missed it?

The Underhill must have muted the natural pull mates felt—but that didn't matter now. All that did was getting to her, finding and catching her, feeling, possessing, claiming—

A raving beast writhed in his chest, outraged that his *cariad* should run from him but also excited by the chase. He saw her ahead, wings fluttering—*why doesn't she fly?*—and decided to end this. Perhaps later, when she was amenable and his, she'd let him chase her again through the forest.

Now, he needed to see and feel and breathe her.

He closed the distance, anticipating when she feinted left but darted right. His arms were there, catching her, pulling her into him, where she belonged.

The feel of her warm skin, her chest expanding with breath, the scent of her hair—glorious. Gavriel clutched her tight, her presence, her very existence, a shock to his body and soul. And under it all, his magick flooded the hollow it'd left behind to tether to the Underhill.

For the first time, he got a good look at his pink maiden. She wasn't merely pink but the color of summer roses, with gold striations. She was smaller than her kin, barely reaching his breastbone, even with her fluttering wings and their little hooked claws at the joint and delicate membrane. Two short, conical horns were nearly lost in the heavy mass of her hair, and precious little claws scratched at him.

She fought him for all her small frame was worth, bucking and boxing him with her wings. Those little claws dug into the leather of his vambraces, and her tail whipped at his boots, trying to unbalance him. She'd had training, his little warrior.

She's perfect. He could see how the druids blended and softened the strength and power of Fomorians with the more pleasing lines of humans to create her kind. Truly, she looked neither human nor Fomorian but something entirely different and wonderful. *Perfect. Mine.*

But as she struggled, Gavriel finally realized it wasn't relief or love or comfort she felt being in his arms. Her terror and anguish radiated from her wide eyes, pupils blown wide in gold irises, and her mouth hung open, baring tiny fangs in a silent howl.

She shoved at him, tucking in close to ram him with a shoulder.

Gavriel hissed through his teeth, and she went rigid feeling the hot bar of his cock pressed between them. A whimper escaped her, the wrong kind, a sound he never wanted her to make ever again.

With a strength and patience he hadn't thought he possessed anymore, Gavriel collected himself, reined back that bestial part of him that saw its mate and wouldn't be satisfied until she was under him. Gavriel would never take what wasn't offered freely, especially not from the one dearest to him.

He hadn't known the pull could so utterly overwhelm him. All the stories made it such a romantic thing, the immediate attraction and recognition. It wasn't supposed to be chasing down a mate and rutting on the forest floor like animals. At least . . . not when one was scared as a rabbit hiding from a wolf.

He gentled his hold but couldn't let go entirely. Gavriel wasn't sure he could ever let her go again, even with the pull of the Underhill twisting like a dagger in his gut.

Her breaths came in gasping sobs that gutted him, and tears overflowed her eyes. Sinking to the ground as dead weight, she made him bend to keep hold of her. She turned her face into the dirt, hair and wings falling around her.

She looked so small, so broken; his ardor withered and the possessiveness inside him gentled, wanting to comfort and protect.

"*Cariad*, please—"

"Just do it," she murmured, "kill me and be done with us."

A tortured groan rumbled through him. He knelt beside her, drawing her off the ground to cradle against his chest and tuck her head under his chin. Her hair was matted with sweat from running and saturated in her scent. He just stopped himself from burying his nose between her horns and taking a long draught of her—lavender and cream and sunshine. He shuddered, wanting to fill himself up on the scent.

"No!" She squirmed, believing the worst of him.

"I'd sooner cast myself to the Otherworld than harm you, *cariad*." He loosened his hold but couldn't let her go. "Please, I know you've no reason to trust me, but I vow that you will never come to harm."

She laughed joylessly, still wriggling in his grip. "You say this after what your kind did to mine?" she hissed. "Their blood hasn't even gone cold."

He grimaced, his shame nearly eclipsing the joy of finding her.

"I took no part, but . . . I couldn't stop it." He, a general, one of the strongest fae warriors, had been powerless to stop the slaughter, was unable to undo the night's tragedy or ease the anguish of his mate. His bottomless pit of guilt and shame widened.

"I should've been here, with them."

He shook his head vehemently.

"I was supposed to be here," she continued tonelessly, her eyes glassy and unseeing. She didn't speak to him anymore, but the words came anyway. "Everyone goes to the Gorsedd. But s-she wouldn't—she—"

Hot tears splattered on his arms, burning him to the very core, where his magick pulsed. Where she now ruled.

He held her as her tears watered the ground with her grief. They ate him alive and filled his mind with memories of Faerie, how it had fallen, how he had failed. Her sobs were the sound of an agony so vast, only those who knew what it was lose everything understood.

Gavriel understood.

All he could do was hold her up as she gave her grief voice.

It took a long while to find the end of her tears, and even then, she shuddered with sobs, covering her face with a hand. But after another wobbly breath, he watched her pull the pieces of her heart together and straighten her back.

"You were my friend," she rasped.

"I'll always be your friend. Always."

"Why did . . .?"

"I don't have many answers, and those I do . . . I won't burden your heart with them today."

She turned to look at him for the first time. He held still as she took his measure, searching for something in his face. Disappointment sat bitter on his tongue—what could he hope she'd find there?

"The fae are led by a cruel female," he answered her unspoken question. "She took back the magick used to create your kind to bolster her own."

Her expression hardened. "Then why am I still here? Why was I spared?" She nearly choked on the last word.

"I don't know," he admitted. He rebelled against the thought of her laying alongside her slaughtered kin, yet he couldn't help questioning why she'd escaped.

"I don't want to be spared," she whispered. "The last of my kind. I'm deformed, useless . . ." She shook her head in despair.

"*No*," he growled. "I don't know why—goddess gift, fate, or luck—but you were meant to live, *cariad*, and I'm grateful for it."

She blinked at him with owlishly wide eyes. "I don't know what to do," she murmured, her lower lip trembling, as if the smallest thing, a rabbit rustling or a gentle breeze, would break her all over again.

Gavriel pulled her further into the curve of his body, bringing their faces so close their noses nearly touched. He felt her warm puff of breath on his lips.

"You'll *live*, sweetling, that's what you'll do. You need only live to honor your kin." And he told her all the things she'd do, recounting all the dreams she'd told him through the well. He told her of the places she'd heard stories of and would see with her own eyes. He told her of the things she'd learn from all the people she'd meet. He told her how she'd live the life she dreamed and take her people with her as she did it. He told her how her very existence was a gift.

She regarded him for a long time, long after his words ran out. Gavriel didn't rush her, but the pull of the Underhill grew evermore insistent, a physical wrenching in his chest that nearly crushed the breath from his lungs. He resisted, needing to know that she'd—that she wouldn't—

"It really was you, in the well," she whispered.

The breath caught in his throat as she reached for him, her fingertips brushing his cheek. Achingly slow, her palm cupped his face, the heat of it branding him. He turned his face into the warmth of her hand, soaking in her touch.

"I lived for when you came to see me. *Fy annwyl*, my sunlight," he told her, pressing his lips to her palm.

She gasped . . . but didn't pull away.

"I don't understand," she said.

He thought perhaps she did, a wary knowing in her eyes, but he couldn't ask more of her.

Gavriel covered her hand in his and kissed the palm again before gently lifting and setting her on her feet. He held on as she found her balance, the need to return grinding against his bones, but he stole just a little more time.

He let his head fall to hers and pressed his lips to her temple, his words into her skin. "Tell me your name, sweetling. Please."

On a trembling breath, she whispered, "Carys."

Carys. Cariad. Love, heartmate.

The goddesses were making it obvious for him, it seemed, as if he could miss the way his blood rushed in his ears, a cacophony beating inside him that declared, unequivocally, irrefutably, that he was *hers*.

His lips grazed the shell of her ear to whisper, "I am Gavriel."

To other fae, he was Gavren Gwynvael. Only his mother and the goddess Danu, who whispered it to her upon his birth, knew his true name. True names were jealously guarded by his kind, a goddess gift that could easily be corrupted. Knowing a true name gave a being power over another.

But that was a foregone end. This lovely creature already held his heart in her little clawed fist. While the Underhill may claim his body and magick, everything else was hers.

He tried to keep the grimace from his face as the Underhill's pull turned into thousands of gnashing teeth, biting at his back.

"I must go," he admitted, hating the words.

Her brows jumped, panic suffusing her face.

Gavriel clutched her hands, running his thumbs over the broken skin of her knuckles and fingertips. With the burst of his returned magick, he healed every cut and splinter, knitting the skin back together. She watched silently, her eyes wide.

He kissed her palms and every healed fingertip. "Wherever you are, if you call, I'll come, *cariad*. This I vow to you."

He knew they were promises he likely couldn't keep, but he made them anyway.

Finally, Gavriel could fight the pull no longer. Magick buzzed around him, moving his limbs for him faster than even a fae could naturally muster. The Underhill claimed him, for now. But he left behind his heart, his name, and his promise. Everything that mattered.

Eight

Carys returned to her mother's house. She'd told her ghost she wouldn't go back, but that promise had been made in another life by another female, one whose heart wasn't shattered with grief.

Everything was just as Arda left it, herbs drying from the rafters, dough left to prove, a half-finished set of freshly fletched arrows. And the rockfall that had led to Carys's chambers. She stared at it for a long while, anger simmering in her belly just above that heavy, numbing grief that smothered everything else. That she couldn't reach her own things made her angry, what her mother did made her angry, being angry at her slaughtered mother made her angry, and having a slaughtered mother at all made her angry. Guilt rode hard on the heels of all that anger, forming a hot knot in her throat that wouldn't budge.

But she'd cried enough, so Carys swallowed those tears, deep down where she couldn't feel it or anything else, and escaped into mindless activity.

She gathered everything she could, making a pile in the front room. But when night fell, she took shelter in another dwelling, unable to bear sleeping alone in her mother's home.

Morning came cold and gray, a reminder of all that had happened and been lost. Carys collected everything she could from the clanhomes, everything useful, everything dear. At first she thought to take it with her . . . somewhere. Somewhere they would be safe and cherished, to keep the memories alive.

But on the second day, when the pile grew taller than her, she realized her folly. What use did she have for old heirlooms and pretty baubles? Nothing would bring their owners back nor keep their memories alive.

So she buried all the dear, meaningful things along with her sentiment and her memories in a cave deep in the clanhome for safekeeping.

On the third day, she packed as many useful things as she could and headed north. The clanhome was a home no longer but a skeleton, bereft of its heart. Carys left hers behind, for whatever little use it was, already broken beyond repair.

It took a fortnight to find a suitable place. She'd never been this far north into Eryri; only a few clans had made their homes so far from Caerdyf. She left behind all the places she knew on the second day of travel, never lingering long in those other empty clanhomes. If she did, she began to wonder which inhabitants had become rock and which were now rot. So Carys pushed on. And didn't think.

She avoided human settlements, unsure if the Pritani would welcome her, useless as she was, or if they'd even been spared from the fae.

She followed the coast, content to let her feet decide where to go. The landscape changed around her, rising in stark green hills and valleys, but she barely saw. Carys watched her feet, her footfalls a steady rhythm that kept everything inside, everything down.

She didn't feel the cold or her chapped lips. She didn't feel the knots in her hair or her shoulders. The only thing that bothered her was the blisters, but they didn't stop her.

Her feet eventually led her inland, following the rivers. It was only when she slipped on smooth river rocks, talons scrabbling for purchase, that Carys finally looked up.

A thin lake stretched out before her, the water dark and cold. Severe, craggy hills hemmed either side, creating a steep valley dominated by the lake. At the far side, the lake narrowed into a river again and disappeared into the forest, but where Carys stood, a beach of pebbles gently sloped into the water. Up a small berm stood a copse of trees, protected on two sides by thick berry bushes.

Carys dug her talons into the pebbles.

It'll do.

By the time spring grew into summer, Carys was sick of berries. She'd gorged on all the ripe ones, staining her hands and chin, not caring since who was there to see her. No one. Just the birds.

She spent her days fighting the birds away from her berry bushes, waiting for the green fruit to ripen. Guarding them against roving beaks became her obsession.

Can't even scare away birds. Useless, said a voice so like her mother's.

She was so hungry those first days, but she could ignore the hunger pangs—at least until she went woozy, then she finally relented and ate some of the food she'd brought with her. Eventually, the berries and food from the clanhome ran out and her stomach learned to make do with less.

She'd been spoiled, living in a community where there were always hands to help. It took her days to grind down roots and seeds. She cried when she hunted her first rabbit, cried as she roasted and ate every bit, cried for how delicious it was, and cried when her stomach wanted more.

She cried for her second and third rabbit, too. Then she cried when she didn't feel so badly about the fourth but felt she should.

Eventually, her tears ran out for the rabbits, just as they'd run out for her kin. With nothing left inside, no tears, no hope, the numbness took her again, and she was grateful. It was easier to just exist, to fill her stomach when she could and sleep the days and nights away. At least in sleep she could escape the grief and loneliness.

In the thick summer heat, Carys realized it wouldn't be enough to just exist. When all the easily attainable food ran out and the last of her arrows disappeared in the underbrush, she went days without eating. She considered just sleeping until hunger and thirst did their work, but something inside her, a quicksilver spark of stubbornness refused to lay down and die.

So Carys took her hand-axe and cut branches to make a proper shelter. She whittled new arrow shafts and repurposed the clothing and leathers she'd brought. She dried meat and cured skins. And when the heat grew too great, she sat in the lake on a flat rock she found. Sometimes she washed herself, scraping away days of grime and sweat, or she waited for the fish to come nibble at her and caught the slowest in her claws.

By the time summer waned, she was sick of fish, too, but it didn't matter, she ate or smoked everything she caught. Carys didn't know how much she'd need nor what the winter would bring. She didn't let herself think on it, just started building food stores knowing she'd need them.

Perhaps it was foolish, but Carys didn't think—of herself, of her situation, of the future. And certainly never about the face she sometimes saw in the water.

She'd spotted it in late spring, a glimmer not unlike fish scales. She didn't let herself wonder about it, didn't look too hard to see if it truly was the same face that'd peered at her from a well, a lifetime ago.

If she let herself think of *him*, she'd have to feel that odd tugging in her chest, one that reminded her of the recognition she'd felt in his arms, a dizzying rightness she refused to believe.

It was the pain of losing everything, she told herself. She'd cleaved to the first familiar person, seeking comfort.

She missed him, she could admit that, missed their conversations and friendship, but she missed her sisters too and her clan. She missed her former life, even if it included her mother.

So whether or not it was *his* face she saw didn't matter—he couldn't be what she'd thought in a moment of madness and grief, and she made peace with never having what she'd longed for. That dream had died along with all her kin.

Carys would have no dreams, no mate, no people. Nothing but her life. And when winter came, perhaps she wouldn't even have that.

Nine

Gavriel hadn't known it was possible for his heart to break over and over again. To know his *cariad*, his Carys, existed at all kept him going, and the sight of her soothed him just enough to manage another day. He'd nearly gone mad when he couldn't see her, scraping his fingers raw more than once trying to claw his way out. Finding another rift, one near the shore of the lake she'd claimed, was a stroke of luck that smacked of the divine, but Gavriel wasn't fool enough to question it, not when it gifted him the sight of his mate and a tenuous thread of sanity.

But it was its own kind of curse. At first she'd grown dirty and haggard, the lush curves he thought of every time he tried to sleep wasting away to rangy muscle. Then she'd slept her days away, rarely offering him the opportunity to spot her. He took a little heart when she pulled herself up, cleaned herself off, and began to hunt and fish and *survive*.

He longed for her to see him in the water, to call his name, even if he didn't know what would happen. But she never looked for him. She barely looked anywhere but right in front of her.

Gavriel saw no light in her eyes. Just as he'd come alive again, his magick and vitality buzzing inside him in a way it hadn't since being tethered to the Underhill, he watched his mate wither away.

It wasn't enough anymore to wait and pine in the dark, knowing she was out there, alone and hurting.

It didn't matter anymore that all fae were bound to the Underhill, knowing so long as he was here, he wasn't where he should be—with *her*.

Gavriel hadn't defeated the Fomorians. He hadn't protected his people or queen. But by Danu and any other goddess listening, he wouldn't fail his mate.

He spent his forlorn days hunting the Underhill for weaknesses; it was how he'd found an undiscovered path that led to the rift in the lake. When he wasn't keeping vigil over his *cariad*, he continued his search, barely taking time to rest.

His mate needed him.

He wanted to tell Allarand as much when his friend cautioned him against wandering too far, thinking of course of those they'd lost to the darkness.

"Titania won't come for you," Allarand warned, his brows a heavy shadow over his weary eyes. She hadn't used her new infusion of power to go after anyone at all.

"But she likes me so much," Gavriel grumbled back, not stopping his circuit but making Allarand walk with him.

Allarand stopped short, staring at him. "I can't remember the last time you joked."

"Probably not worth remembering. It was a poor one anyhow."

His friend grunted in agreement and fell into step beside him. Out here, so far from the hive, he could speak more freely. Allarand kept Gavriel appraised of what transpired in court—or rather, what didn't.

The Hunt had returned drunk on the reclaimed magick. Titania was so saturated in it, a faint purple aura outlined her. She and her favorites had spent countless days indulging in the power, warping crystals, turning mounts into other creatures, and indulging in all manner of debaucheries. Gavriel had fled into the darkness, but Allarand kept close to court, always pressing his end when Titania was lucid.

"I doubt she means to share the magick," Allarand growled, falling into step with Gavriel as he made another circuit, looking, searching.

"It should be given to Rhiannon."

"Instead, they gorge themselves for a moment's pleasure." Allarand spat the words, but Gavriel couldn't quite share his outrage.

Gavriel shared his friend's sentiment but couldn't deny the lure of a moment's pleasure. Those few moments he'd stolen with Carys often repeated in his mind, the memories unspooling anytime his thoughts wandered away from his mission. He'd tried to gorge himself on the sight, smell, feel of her, and they sustained him.

It was easy to sink into the pleasure of those memories, tainted as they were with tragedy, but they made him long for more. Much, much more.

"*Y*ou need to be more discreet with your inquiries," said Allarand many days later.

Gavriel arched a brow but didn't slow his pace.

"Titania grows bored with playing sorceress. If you aren't careful, you'll draw her attention asking strange questions."

Gavriel nodded his thanks. "I'll be more careful, my friend."

"Why exactly are you asking elders about the magick used to make the creatures?"

He grimaced, knowing Allarand would eventually try to suss out answers.

"It's odd, don't you think, that the magick could be taken in the first place," Gavriel hedged.

"Yes . . . but it was magick imbued there long before our time."

"But we all felt when it was taken. It was connected to us but existed outside the Underhill."

"And now it's trapped with us."

"Yes, but somehow, humans were able to harness it. Untether it." He heard the frantic fervor in his own voice and knew Allarand did too at the disturbed look he cast Gavriel.

"Some are saying . . ." Allarand's mouth twisted uncomfortably, "you ask about matings between fae and *others*."

There was no question voiced, but as Allarand stopped to regard him gravely, it lay between them all the same.

He couldn't answer the worry in his friend's eyes, but he could allay it.

"I swear to you, what I do affects only me. I won't put our people in danger."

Allarand laid a heavy hand on Gavriel's shoulder, making him stop. "*You* are our people, too, Gavren. And my friend. Fae are still disappearing."

Gavriel clasped Allarand's forearm, moved by his friend's worry. "I'll be careful," he promised. He'd no intention of courting danger or disaster. But he'd promised his mate his heart, his troth, and his protection. Perhaps not in words spoken, but promised just the same. He couldn't make good on them from down here in the darkness.

So Gavriel was careful with his inquiries and who he made them to, but he remained dogged in his pursuit. He avoided Titania and her minions. He stood watch over his mate and stole every glimpse of her he could. He roamed the Underhill until he'd forged whole new paths that led nowhere.

But as summer waned in Albion, he was no closer to outwitting the Underhill or getting to his mate than when he'd tried to claw his way out. Sharp hooks of despair tried to pull him under; all the questions had been asked, all the paths had been tread. His magick and strength thrummed like a second pulse, that possessive beast inside him howling to be with his mate, tired of being caged. Desperate to do *something*.

The frustration ate him alive—there had to be something . . . even if it was clawing the barrier down to his bones.

Ten

The day settled into dusk as Carys followed a deer-path through the forest, the quail she'd caught bouncing on her hip. The weather had turned a fortnight ago, the nights cooling enough that Carys buried herself beneath every blanket, cloak, and unworn tunic. She'd begun filling the holes and cracks of her twig shelter with mud from the lake, to keep a bit of her own warmth inside.

She had a little time yet, but as the mornings grew crisp and damp, she couldn't help but worry. Whatever time she didn't spend hunting or foraging she devoted to hiding her store from scavengers. The squirrels and birds were a nuisance; it was the wolves that worried her.

The thought of them made her stomach churn, and she hurried back to the lake.

Some days, returning to her little hovel on the lake was a relief, the sight familiar and safe and full of all her worldly things. But others, it filled her with a despondency that was hard to shake. Her life had never been grand, but on some days, she looked at her twig house and nest of fraying blankets and couldn't help thinking of her old chamber in her mother's house.

Thinking of that room made her think of her mother, but Carys didn't like thinking of her, split between grief and anger. So she thought of her sisters instead and all the others of her clan. She missed the safety and noise of the clanhome, the bustle of everyday existence. There had always been something cooking, someone talking, a friendly ear. Whenever she'd been ill, or when winter set in, the clan had been there to weather it.

As she neared the lake, a forlorn ache bloomed in her chest, and hot tears pricked her eyes.

She'd taken her clan for granted, had thought that because of her wings and being mateless, she was alone.

That naïve female didn't know the meaning of loneliness.

What she wouldn't give now for her kin and her life before. Even if it meant never having a mate. Even if it meant living with her mother's abuses. And even if it meant never seeing *him* again.

Thoughts of *him* were hardest to stop. The memories of his face, his hands, his smell were the only spots of brightness in a day that had ripped her world apart. Even now, when her mind weakened late in the night, tired and heartsick, those fleeting memories offered her a little comfort.

Those afternoons spent with him, calling down the sound of birds and shapes of clouds, had filled her heart and life with warmth, burning away her loneliness then. As she lay there, alone in her hovel, thoughts of *him* made her heart beat a little faster . . .

Stop. She had to stop—

Rough male voices snagged her attention. Two figures lurked outside her shelter, passing her things between them. Carys watched, frozen, as they pointed at her blankets, her tools, her food, clearly arguing over who would get what.

Her chest seized when they looked up and saw her, still halfway between the forest and her shelter. Her pulse drummed in her ears, deafening, warning, as the figures looked between them then at her. They dropped her things and took a step closer.

Two human men leered at her through the dim dusk, one tall and one short, both rangy with unwashed hair and tattered tunics. The bones of their faces were too prominent, their eyes too wide and bright.

"Well, now," said the tall one. "Didn't think I'd see one of them again."

"Thought they all died," agreed the shorter one.

"Didn't know some were so small, so . . ." Carys felt the tall one's eyes run down her body as surely as if it was his hand, and she shivered in disgust.

The crude flick of his tongue across his lips broke her frightened daze.

She pulled out her favorite dagger. "You need to leave," she said, just keeping the tremble from her voice.

The short one smiled, baring his yellowed teeth. "C'mon, sweetling, share with us."

"I'm not your sweetling. Go back the way you came."

The tall one scratched his scruffy cheek. "See now, we can't do that. Got some bad men looking for us. Needed to find somewhere to lie low, and look what we found."

Carys flexed her talons and fluffed her wings to seem bigger. Their overbright eyes watched her every move, though the sight of her wingclaws and lashing tail made them hesitate.

These were dangerous, hungry men with nothing to lose, and it was too dangerous in the forest at night to turn and run, and if she did, they'd be on her in a moment. Her wings would be easy to grab, an easy way to hold her down.

Bile burned her throat thinking of being held down by these two, of what they'd do once they got her there.

She brandished her dagger again, but the men kept coming.

The tall one lunged first, bony hands going for her throat. The second came right behind, grabbing for the dagger.

Carys blocked the first with her wing, slicing across his face with her wingclaw, and slashed at the second with her blade.

She danced back a few paces, keeping them in her sight, as each cradled their bleeding wounds.

"That was a warning," she growled. "Leave."

The shorter man's lip pulled back, not in a smile this time but a snarl.

"You're going to regret that, sweetling," he hissed.

"When we're through with—"

Thwunk went her dagger, straight into the tall man's shoulder. He yowled in pain, but his companion charged her as she drew her knife. She had it out but not up in time before she went crashing down under the shorter man.

They scuffled in the dirt, fighting for her knife. The man smashed his hand into her face, and blood gushed from her nose. Carys dug her claws into his side where he was soft, clutching for organs, and made him screech.

"Help me, you fucking fool!" he screamed.

"She stabbed me!"

"Then return the favor!"

Carys tried every trick, constricting her tail around his leg, boxing his ears with her wings, even sinking the wingclaws into his shoulders—but he was strong in his desperation. He grunted but kept his seat, one hand clamped around her wrist with the knife and the other going for her throat.

A foot landed on her left wing, and Carys keened in pain as a bone splintered.

The tall one loomed over her, eyes dark with malice, and spat on her.

"Hold still," growled the short man, "or we'll kill you."

"Slowly," the other added.

They'd be saving winter the trouble, really. But a hot, desperate part of her refused to lay down and die. *Not like this.* Not violated in the dirt by these worms.

She may not want her lonely existence, but she didn't want to die like this.

If she was to meet her kin in the next life tonight, it would be in a way that made them proud—with a weapon in her hand, her claws bloody, and her talons beneath her.

Carys struck, fangs sinking into the meat of his forearm. He jerked in surprise, easing off just enough for her to knee him in the back. He lurched forward, into her free wing and the claw she slashed across his face and neck. Blood splattered her face as he slumped off, clutching his throat.

The tall man roared, lifting her dagger above his head, but she rolled away. He scrambled to pull the blade from where he'd buried it in the ground, but Carys was quicker, raking her claws across his chest.

He fell back with a heavy thud, the shorter man tripping over his flailing arms.

Still gripping his bleeding neck, the shorter one gurgled, "G-go!" and the two of them staggered into the darkness, their breaths labored and overloud. Every predator for miles would hear them and smell their blood.

Carys crouched there with a blade in either hand, ready for an ambush or trick, until the moon hung high and bright in a clear sky. Only when the forest creatures' nightly sounds began to echo through the trees did she turn on shaky legs for the lake.

She staggered into the water, limbs unsteady and broken wing throbbing. She fell to her knees, the cold water divine against her hot, broken skin. Plunging her face in, she scrubbed at the blood and spit tangled in her hair.

Carys ran her hands over her face, assessing the swelling bruises and cuts. Her nose hadn't been broken, but all the scratches and cuts would require the last of her tincture. Her wings sank into the water, too exhausted to stay upright.

In the warm cavern of her palms, Carys cried. First came hiccupping sobs for her wounds, stinging and sore. Then came salty tears, her terror and panic leaking from her eyes. Next came wails, long reverberations of anguish that echoed across the surface of the lake, the sound of a soul who had just cheated death but still couldn't believe it. Then, finally, heaving gasps that stole her breath and stabbed at her chest as surely as her loneliness, as deep as the lake around her.

So close. If I'd died, who would know?

She sank deeper in the water, too numb to feel the chill of the water. Wrapping her arms around herself, she tried to keep everything together and inside when all she wanted to do was come apart.

For just a moment, she wanted to lay her head on someone's shoulder and set down her burdens. She wanted more than just two wretched humans to know she still existed.

Just for a moment, she wanted to not be alone.

Carys wiped at her tears, and for the first time looked for *his* face in the lake.

For the first time, she said his name.

"Gavriel . . ."

Eleven

The lake bubbled and churned, and the world seemed to bend around Carys, tearing and cracking to reveal shafts of blinding light. The air sizzled, her nose burning with the smell of petrichor, as a rip tore through the very space before her. From the tear a figure stumbled into the water, a groan on their lips. It was over in a moment, flashing like a comet and then burning out in a haze.

Steam wafted off the figure as they staggered closer.

Carys stared at a pair of finely worked leather boots encasing a set of strong knees. Her eyes traveled up muscled thighs clad in soft wool, to a dark velvet tunic, cinched at a narrow waist by a belt of exquisitely tooled silver. The tunic spread taut over a wide chest, heaving for breath. A sapphire cape, edged in silver thread, fell from one shoulder.

A male fae, impossibly beautiful and glowing with his own silver light under the pale moon, stared back at her, his finely formed lips parted and quicksilver eyes wide in astonishment. His opalescent skin and the silver rings dangling from the long, delicate points of his ears glinted in the moonlight.

Gavriel.

"You're here," she croaked.

"So I am," he said slowly, the rich timber of his voice making some-thing deep inside her settle. "But I don't understand . . ." He looked down at her, eyes almost dazed. "You called for me. Said my name."

"Yes. And you came . . . like you said you would."

His mouth opened, but nothing came out. He took in the dark lake, a looking glass reflecting the glittering stars and bright moon ringed in a halo of blue . . . and then her, still slumped in the water.

"*Fy annwyl,* you . . ."

A sharp inhale, and then he was plucking her from the water and carrying her to shore, wrapped tight in his arms.

Carys let her head fall to his shoulder. She drew in the scent of him, woody and rich, and the feel of him surrounding her almost made her want to weep again.

The tumult of the day nearly overwhelmed her, the gamut of emo-tions more than she'd allowed herself to feel in months, but as his warmth suffused her, there was one that surpassed all the rest.

Rightness.

It was exactly as the elders said it would be, a knowing, a reunion, a settling of all the pieces.

Heartsong.

More tears did escape, but this time from sheer, impossible, utter relief. In his arms, the loneliness finally ebbed enough for Carys to *breathe.*

She grumbled when he set her on her feet, not wanting to leave the comfort of his arms, but he was determined to look her over. She held still as he searched for hurts. His eyes flashed, dangerous and sharp, when he saw the blood.

"You're wounded."

"It's not all mine."

He went perfectly still, eyes unblinking as he searched her face. "What's happened, *cariad?*"

She shook her head, mouth suddenly dry, and told him of the men. As she spoke, his lip pulled back, carving harsh lines across his cheeks like a hissing feline and revealing his fangs. Though smaller than a male guardian's fangs, the sharp points seemed out of place in such a refined, beautiful face, but Carys liked them, liked that he had a pair to match hers.

"Where are they now?" he asked, eyes already searching the trees.

He made toward the forest, to join all the other predators likely following the trail of blood, but Carys clutched his arm, claws digging into the softness of his tunic.

"Please don't leave me," she said, hating how small she sounded but needing him to stay.

The rigid fury eased from his face as he reached to unclasp the brooch at his right shoulder. His cape was soft and light as silk as he drew it around her shoulders. He pinned the brooch in place at her throat as Carys melted into the softness.

Still, she couldn't help grimacing at the slight weight on her throbbing wing. His quicksilver eyes saw everything, and his lips thinned into an unhappy line at her pain.

"My wing's broken," she said.

"I hope you dealt them even worse."

She blinked in surprise. "I think I did."

"Good."

A bloom of pleasure unfurled in her chest, warming her as surely as his cloak.

She let him look at her cracked knuckles, bruising arms, and tender nose, unsure whether this was all just a dream as he smoothed his fingers over her hurts and took them away with a touch and his magick. Her bruises faded and her cuts knit back together before her eyes.

Just like that day.

He'd done this before, that horrible day, healed her shredded hands. She'd been too distraught to notice then, had only realized days later when she nicked herself on an arrowhead.

Her throat clogged with more tears as he drew her injured wing out from under the cloak, carefully running his hands up the bone. No one had touched her wings since she was small; they'd made many of her clan uneasy. His hands were sure and gentle as he probed the break, holding her steady while his magick flowed.

With a snap that startled her more than hurt, the bone reformed.

Her mouth fell open in amazement, but she quickly frowned to see him cradling his left forearm to his chest.

He explained, "It's faster to just take the wound. I heal quickly."

"You . . . you took the break yourself?"

Carys laid her hand gently on his chest, careful not to jostle him, and he covered it with his, tangling their fingers.

"Yes."

"But . . . why?"

Those quicksilver eyes sparkled like diamonds in candlelight. "Because it's a mate's due."

Her stomach swooped and her heart fluttered.

Mates. The word flitted across her mind like dragonflies on a pond. That she felt this pull, that he felt it too . . . it was everything she did and didn't want. How could she ever love or trust a fae after what his kind had done to hers? But then again, how could she deny the way her heart felt fuller, as if it was finally the right shape?

Perhaps some of it was her loneliness and how dearly she missed her friend in the well. She couldn't deny that either. But it felt like more, had even stirred on that horrible day, when she'd had no ability to acknowledge or comprehend it.

Gavriel must have taken her silence as a bad omen. He fell to a knee, her hand still clutched to his chest. Like this, she was taller than him, but barely, and she stared down at him in surprise.

"I don't mean to scare you, *fy annwyl,* but I must tell you the truth. I've been drawn to you from the moment you peered down at me through the well. I knew why when I saw you across that glen You are *cariad,* my mate. My people are blessed by the goddesses with only one, and you are mine."

He turned her hand over and kissed the palm, the heat of his lips searing her and his words pouring over her like syrup, sweet and thick.

"I don't deserve you or your forgiveness, but I've waited for you for thousands of these mortal years, and I'm not a good male. I want you for my own, my *cariad*. I want your sweetness, your smiles, your burdens. I would take them all and pledge my troth to you, if you'd have me." He looked up at her again, so hopeful, so fearful, to say, "Please tell me you feel it, too."

Carys's heart lurched into her throat, the joy and weight of such words heavy to bear.

What could he see in you, deformed and useless? He says he wants your burdens, but what happens when he realizes you're the burden?

She hated these thoughts in her mother's voice. She hated that she questioned the words she'd waited so long to hear.

He was fae, and she was useless.

Yet . . . he'd warned her of the danger and took her wounds into himself. He prostrated himself before her and asked forgiveness for evils that weren't his own, his ethereally beautiful face proud as he awaited judgment that wasn't his to bear.

And she . . . she was the last of her kind, a small guardian with small fangs and small horns and malformed wings. She was dirty and unkempt, painfully so beside his elegance—but she was also a guardian who'd defended herself against two attackers. One who'd kept herself alive, with nothing and no one.

That has to count for something, she thought.

Something shifted inside her, something just as profound as the mate pull.

If she could think that . . . perhaps she could believe this proud fae warrior when he said she was the one he'd waited for.

Drawing in a breath and all her courage, Carys said, "I feel it, too."

He was up faster than she could see, hands in her hair. "*Cariad,*" he whispered, like it was a promise.

His eyes fell to her lips, but he didn't claim that last small distance, waiting.

Carys cupped his face, the cool gleam of his skin belying the heat radiating from him. With the slightest pressure from her fingertips, she drew him down to her.

His lips slid against hers and locked into place, a feeling so perfect she couldn't help her moan of pleasure. Barely a touch and it was already so much better than all the things she'd done with a few males in her clan.

Gavriel tipped up her chin with a crooked finger, deepening the kiss. She gasped when he canted her head just so and swooped inside, tangling their tongues. It was as though the heat and power of him seeped inside her and filled all the little cracks and voids.

Carys lost herself in the slick slide of his tongue and sharp points of his fangs. His arms wrapped around her and lifted, taking her weight and bringing their mouths even. Carys threw her arms around his shoulders and sank a hand into the heavy curtain of his silky starlight hair. He groaned at the light scrape of her claws along his head, and she felt the noise deep in her center, a place she hadn't thought of in a very long time.

But now, with just a few kisses, it was all she could think about.

Gavriel pressed searing kisses to her cheeks, brows, nose, and throat, his fangs scraping with his tongue just behind to soothe. She writhed in his arms, hooking her legs around his lean hips to bring them flush together.

"I burn for you, *cariad*," he whispered roughly against her lips before claiming them again, devouring her.

Burning, that's what this felt like, combusting from the inside out. Her desire had never been so intense before, and a niggle of fear skirted her mind, that she was so quickly being consumed by the mate bond, with a fae no less—but then Gavriel filled a hand with her backside, drawing her impossibly closer, as if he could fuse them together, and Carys was lost again.

But being lost to their bond didn't feel like a loss, not when he pressed kisses to her skin and growled rough promises in her ear. How even from down in the well he'd been transfixed by her mouth and imagined all the ways she'd use it for him. How he'd waited a thousand years for her and it would take another thousand to do everything he wanted to her. How the Underhill and its darkness was nothing to her sunlight.

She felt all his urgency and longing in his kisses and the firm grip of his hands; it was a companion to her own but evermore vast, centuries of loneliness she couldn't fathom condensed into a single moment of unbridled relief. She tasted it on his tongue, that relief, and something sweetly spicy, too, like mulled wine and the smallest desperate hope.

Carys kissed him until her lips were swollen and her core thrummed with neediness. She kissed him until she was out of breath and then kissed him more, unable to break away, needing the warmth and pressure and promise of it.

His hands were everywhere except where she burned for him most, driving her mad. As if he could hear her growing need, he widened his stance and kissed along her jaw to her ear, where he whispered in a rumbling, lyrical purr, "Could I make my mate come for me just like this, I wonder?" She felt his smile against her skin, the points of his fangs teasing along her neck.

"You could try and see," she whispered back.

She didn't know where the words or the bravery to say them came from, but she was rewarded when his big body shuddered and he fixed her with eyes that promised dark, delicious things. A slow, wicked smile overtook his face and stole her breath. She'd thought him merely beautiful before; with that lopsided grin and the dimples it revealed, he was truly breathtaking.

"Oh, *cariad*," he said in a velvety rumble. "Shall I start with all the ways I'll—"

Gavriel doubled over with a pained grunt, taking Carys with him. She yelped and clung to him, her hair and wings brushing the ground before he got hold of himself and staggered upright. He let her down gently, and her lust quelled at the sight of his grimace.

Whatever it was seemed to pass after a few long moments; eventually, his shoulders eased and he sighed in relief.

"It seems I don't have time, love. At least, not *enough* time," he said with a sad smile.

"What *was* that?" she demanded, checking him over now.

He caught her roving hands and pressed them to his chest. "My kind is trapped in the Underhill. We tethered ourselves to it, and it won't let go."

"But you're here?"

Gavriel nodded, his eyes dark and distant, as if he was just as perplexed. "We can leave for a short time if there's enough power to break the barrier. I've only ever known a royal high fae to be strong enough to do it. But you . . . you used my true-name." He gazed down at her in wonder. "My mate calling my true-name was enough to break the barrier."

She opened her mouth, to tell him it couldn't be that simple, when Gavriel staggered again. She set her feet and took his weight, keeping him upright.

"Then what's happening?" she wanted to know when the pain passed.

"I'm called back," he said, looking grimly at the lake. "I'm still tethered to the Underhill."

"If the tether's so strong, why did saying your name do anything at all?"

He smiled at her gently, carding his fingers through her hair. "Because you used my true-name. The one bestowed by Danu herself. Names have power over my kind."

A knot of emotion tugged at her throat. "You gave me yours that day."

"Yes. And I'd give you everything else, *cariad*, everything I am. You command me, body and soul. And it was enough to free me from the Underhill."

"Not truly, though. Not for good," she said, heart sinking, feeling as though she'd already failed him.

Gavriel drew her into his arms, and she buried her face against his chest. She could hear his heart, strong and steady, and let the rhythm soothe her.

"It's a start, *cariad*. I can feel my magick growing. Something's begun." He nuzzled her hair. "I want a life with you, Carys, if you'll have me. If that means challenging the Underhill, then so be it."

The weight of his hope settled on Carys's shoulders, heavy and terrifying.

Send him away now, before he gets hurt when you fail.

Carys turned her face up, savoring each fluttering kiss he bestowed on her forehead, nose, cheeks, and lips.

This male had given her his name, his protection, his hopes. It may be terrifying, but she was honored to carry them all.

"There must be a way," she said.

Gavriel sighed happily, humming his agreement before he took her mouth in another of those intoxicating kisses that pulled her under quicker than an undertow.

There were no more words that night; promises and hopes were enough as they soaked in the comfort of the other's touch, girding themselves for when, inevitably, Gavriel could no longer fight the pull. He kissed her hands before wading into the lake and letting the Underhill reclaim him.

He disappeared in a flash of light just as brilliant as the one that brought him, leaving Carys alone on the shore . . . wrapped in his cloak.

Twelve

Gavriel waited as the handmaid slipped inside Queen Rhiannon's bower. He kept his gaze forward, on the ornate iron door that emerged seamlessly from the surrounding rock, but felt the assessing gaze of the other handmaids. None were keen to allow him inside.

He'd requested more than once to see the queen when she was strong enough but had been met each time with a fierce protectiveness. Gavriel didn't begrudge them that, but he had his own dear one to protect now.

In the days since being pulled from the Underhill by his mate, Gavriel had barely stopped to rest, trying to find a way back to her. They spoke often through the rift, but when she tried to use his name again, though he felt a compulsion, the Underhill's grip on him was stronger.

His impatience grew as surely as his magick, pulsing and itchy under the skin. He'd exhausted everything he knew to try; none of his inquiries with the older fae had garnered anything useful. Finally, seeing no other way, Gavriel sent a gentle query along the tie that every fae had to their Faerie Queen, faint though it was in her sleep.

A begrudging handmaid fetched him two days later.

The iron door opened without so much as a creak, and a slim, pearlescent hand beckoned him inside.

He nodded respectfully to the other handmaidens, all standing vigil still. A warning to him.

Gavriel entered the bower, uneasy at how wary the queen's retinue had become. So jealously guarding her . . . did they fear for the queen's safety?

Though, as he drew close to Rhiannon, perhaps he could understand.

Laid upon a bed of silk, Rhiannon the Gold was resplendent and still. Her long ringlets of golden hair spilled across embroidered pillows, her visage easy as if in sleep. She was immaculate in a dressing gown of lilac silk, but her cheeks were too prominent and her skin lacked the pearlescent gleam of a healthy female fae.

It pained him to see his old friend like this. Gracious in manner and generous to a fault, she was deeply loved by her people. While her spoiled niece sat like a hive queen on the throne, keeping a few chosen close while treating the others like worthless drones, Rhiannon was the spoke, the center of a circle. She supported them, united them, helped them create a more powerful whole.

Looking at his queen now, Gavriel realized that center had gone hollow—Rhiannon was wasting away in whatever duel she waged against the Underhill.

"None of the magick taken on Beltane was returned to her?" Gavriel asked the handmaid.

From her post on the other side of the bower, the handmaid frowned at him. "Lady Titania has found other uses for it," she said, diplomatic but vicious.

He nodded. Another battle to fight in the court, amongst themselves. If the Underhill didn't consume them, they would soon consume each other.

And all the loss and sacrifice will have been for nothing.

No, whispered a voice. Not his own.

The breath hitched in his chest. *Rhiannon.*

"She wishes to speak to you," said the handmaid.

"How—?"

The handmaid wrapped a gentle hand around Rhiannon's wrist and closed her eyes. Gavriel stared raptly as the female trembled, her outline glowing faintly. When she looked at him again, gold light spilled from her eyes, leaving no iris or pupil. A shiver skittered down Gavriel's back, feeling the power of that gaze.

"Rhiannon."

"It's been too long, Gavren," said the handmaid in Rhiannon's voice. She offered a small smile, a gesture he knew so well as hers, a sort of apology when she surprised someone with the vastness of her powers.

Throat choked with emotion, he croaked, "My lady queen."

"Oh, Gavren." Another of her smiles played at her lips, all humor and her favorite to deploy against him. She'd often called him dour and enjoyed teasing him for it. "If you came more often, we'd have time for such niceties, but I cannot hold this connection long. And you've come with grave tidings, I take it. You always do. Give me your report, general." She said this kindly, and Gavriel appreciated her directness.

Clasping his hands behind him, Gavriel recounted everything for Rhiannon. He kept his explanations succinct, the familiarity of a general reporting to his queen allowing him to speak of his mate and his separation from her without succumbing to the desperate beast, consumed by frustration, in his chest.

Rhiannon sighed. "It seems my niece has been quite the little fool."

"The magick she took should be returned to you."

"It's not so simple, I'm afraid. The magick was imbued into Albion long ago, long enough that it became of Albion. That bond only grew the longer it lived within the creatures."

"But if the magick is no longer fae . . ."

"It cannot be reclaimed, for fae have no claim on it anymore. The humans didn't steal it; they harnessed the most potent elements of their realm—magick, earth, and blood. I've probed the magick, and it feels wholly of Albion. The Underhill may turn against it, too, when it realizes a third realm's magick has gotten inside. My foolish niece."

"How did Titania take it, then?"

"She stole it, of course. With a curse."

Gavriel's guts clenched in disgust. All fae knew what dark, cruel things curses were.

But it would explain why Carys hadn't been turned to stone. Although malevolent and powerful, curses had rules, and one was that the curse had to be heard by its victim. As the only guardian not in the glen that night, his *cariad* escaped.

The most important rule of all, though, was that curses, no matter the size, meaning, or maliciousness, could be broken. Not easily, but it could be done.

His mate wouldn't be the last of her kind. There was hope yet. Excited magick crackled from his hands.

Rhiannon made a considering hum, observing the sparks falling from his fingers.

"I've been wondering about your tether. For moons now it's felt . . . looser. A *cariad* would explain much." Those otherworldly eyes rose to his, and he felt the weight of that gaze as she said, "I've learned many things during my sleep. It allows me to go many places, follow the magick and tethers deep into the Underhill. I've searched all its hidey-holes and inspected all its borders. There may be a way out."

His heart clenched in his chest, not daring to hope yet.

"With the Fomorians gone, the Underhill has been using much of its energy keeping us inside and maintaining its borders. The destruction of Faerie created imbalance in the other six realms, and the Underhill is gathering magick to avoid the same fate. When it feels threatened, it takes fae and claims their magick. But keeping us inside has left it vulnerable. Not by much, not enough to breach from inside, but from the outside . . ."

"Carys was able to call me from the outside. But only the once."

"The Underhill learns. But there are forces even it cannot overcome. Soon, Albion will draw close, and the barrier will be ever so weaker."

Samhain.

"If we are ever to escape the Underhill, it must be from the outside." The handmaid shuddered, the light flickering behind her lids, and her hand on the true Rhiannon's wrist tightened. "I haven't long," she muttered.

With effort, she straightened and levelled him with a grave gaze.

"Listen carefully, Gavren Gwynvael, to your last orders from your queen. A *cariad* on the outside, a creature of Albion magick, can act as your tether. On Samhain, break free of the Underhill, complete the mating rites, and bind yourself to her and to Albion. I don't think it coincidence that our people's fates are now intertwined."

"I won't fail you again," Gavriel promised.

Rhiannon smiled sadly. "You've never failed me, Gavren. But I must ask one more thing. Once free, you must find my sister."

Gavriel's jaw went slack. "Morrígan lives?"

"Yes. She sacrificed herself to our spell and took the eternal sleep. In the chaos of the spell, she was in Albion when the barrier went up. I have only begun to sense her again as her power slowly returns. You must find her and protect her until she can awaken. This is a heavy burden you must bear, the both of you, but return my sister to me, and together we can undo our spell and Titania's curse. There is hope yet for our people and your *cariad's* kin."

Thirteen

Carys watched a full moon rise over Samhain from the lakeshore. Bright white and ringed in blue, it slowly climbed to its zenith, no faster for her urging it to hurry. Her chest seized with worry every time a stray cloud crossed the bright orb, convinced the ritual would be ruined.

Gavriel had assured her, in their many talks through the rift, that weather wouldn't affect the power of Samhain. That it was a full moon this night was rare and would lend a little more power, as all full moons held sway, but that was it. What mattered was that it *was* Samhain, when all the realms orbited close together.

All they needed was the right night and the right words, he'd said.

Carys repeated the ancient words he'd taught her under her breath; they'd been a constant litany in her mind for days.

She buried her nose in the collar of Gavriel's cloak, drawing comfort from the faint smell of him. No matter how cold it became, the cloak always kept her warm. He'd been bemused that it remained in

Albion with her but took it as a sign that their plan would work.

Even if it didn't tonight, he'd assured her, they could try again on Beltane or the next Samhain. They'd try until he was free.

She wouldn't fail him.

They spoke every day through the rift, planning but also simply talking. It was like those lazy afternoons at the well but . . . better. No explanations left unsaid, no questions left unasked. His face was still indistinct in the rippling water and his voice a distant, watery echo, but it filled up her heart and soothed the worst of her loneliness.

He spoke of his life before the Underhill as well as his existence within it. He explained fae magick, how it needed a tether or else it could rip a fae apart in its unbridled power, and how the curse put on her kin could be broken. With the quiet of the lake and his gentle patience, Carys could speak of her kin; she cried for them, cleansing tears that lanced something inside her that had festered for too long. She was able to speak of her hopes to one day be accepted despite her deformed wings. His vehement insistence that she was perfect, from her little horns to her elegant wings to her taloned toes, had made her heart thump in a way it never had before.

Carys now lived for when his face appeared in the water and she could speak to her male.

Her mate.

She didn't want to wait and try again. She was determined to do this—for him, for her kin. For herself.

***

Like all guardians, Carys knew the moment the realms aligned, her wings tingling. The elders said it was from the magick in them, handed down from the rock-born.

She blew out a breath and shook out her wings to ease her nerves.

In a voice far steadier than she felt, she said, "Gavriel."

For one horrible moment, nothing happened, and her stomach swooped.

Then a blinding rip split the world, bursts of magick sparking in the air and fizzing in the water. The heavy smell of petrichor permeated the air as a figure appeared, boots sloshing in the shallow water. Then the doorway between worlds collapsed with a hiss of steam.

It'd made little noise, but Carys's ears rang as if a thunderclap had boomed overhead.

She stared at Gavriel from the shore, a little shocked it'd happened so easily, but then he was striding from the lake and into her waiting arms.

"How I've missed you," he said before claiming her mouth in a searing kiss.

That innate *knowing*, dulled by the barrier, had her trembling in delicious relief to finally feel and smell and taste him again.

She hadn't dreamt it. The pull, the mate bond was real, and he was, too.

Too soon he pulled away.

"Are you ready?" he whispered.

Carys nodded and Gavriel guided her hands to his chest. He kept a loose hold of her wrists and gazed down at her solemnly.

Don't fail. I cannot fail him.

Perhaps sensing her rising dread, his thumbs made soothing little circles on her palms.

"Whatever you do, don't let go," he said.

"Not for anything," she promised.

It was part of his kind's mating ritual, keeping hold of each other as their magick explored and finally tethered itself to a *cariad*. He didn't know what it would be like for her, not a fae, but she had to give his magick time to recognize and accept her.

Time that the Underhill wouldn't want to give them. Gavriel didn't know either what the Underhill would do when it felt the tether to him break, but he'd warned her it may influence him. *Change* him. It couldn't truly hurt her, and Gavriel couldn't hurt her as his *cariad*, but it would try breaking her hold.

And if she let go, even for a moment, the Underhill would snatch him away.

Carys dug her fingers into the velvet of his tunic.

The Underhill couldn't have him. Gavriel was hers.

The thought must have showed on her face, as *his* mouth kicked up in a pleased grin. She'd never seen that grin before, but she wanted to again and again with a fierceness that made her a little braver.

Gavriel began the ritual, reciting words in a language as ancient as the goddesses. She didn't understand them, but she felt every one, the promise and weight of them settling over her in a mantle of warmth.

For one wonderful moment, as Gavriel pledged his troth to her, there was only them, limned in moonlight with the stars witness to their union.

She didn't know the words, but she understood when he pledged himself to her. His voice echoed even after the last word fell from his lips.

Something slid across Carys's skin, fluttering like wings before gathering against her breastbone.

His magick.

She took a deep breath and began her part, those ancient words falling from her lips, light as snowfall but just as powerful.

His grip went tight on her wrists.

Carys steadied herself, ready when a resounding snap reverberated across the lake. He staggered forward, unmoored.

Then the Underhill came for him.

A beastly growl rumbled from Gavriel's chest, and Carys watched in horror as shaggy fur erupted from his skin. Within a moment, she held not her mate but a snarling wolf.

The animal snapped and bit, trying to pull free. Fangs sank into her forearms, and the next ancient word came out in a yelp, but she didn't stop the incantation. She told herself the wounds weren't real, and she kept her hold.

The fur in her fingers suddenly went slick, and Carys scrabbled for purchase as his body lengthened and contorted. A horrible hiss slithered against her ears as a huge snake coiled around her. Trapped, Carys held on as the snake squeezed and writhed. The last words of the ritual came in a wheeze as her chest constricted, but she kept her hold.

The serpent shuddered and shrank, and Carys fell to her knees. She gasped for air, hands seizing around writhing flesh.

Next came a stallion with burning red eyes, whinnying and stamping her beneath his prancing hooves. She took the blows and kept her hold.

Then came a dragon, horned and scaled, his chest glowing red with inner flame. He spit fire at her, and Carys's hands burned where she clutched the rough scales. Tears sluiced down her face, steaming in the heat, but she kept her hold.

The dragon began to melt in her hands, the scales leaking through her fingers, and Carys clutched at molten gold, mindless of how it burned the flesh from her fingers. The smell of charred flesh assailed her nose, choking her, but she kept her hold.

A cool caress ran down her nape, and she willed his magick to hurry and find a way inside.

Magick crackled, Gavriel's form twisting into something new faster than Carys could blink. A violent groan tore from him, the change faster and faster—bear lion lamprey—ripping him apart to form again—bramble spider smoke—and Carys lost sight of him through her tears.

A mighty tremor rumbled under her feet, and the lake behind them sloshed. The world seemed to shiver, and Carys's heart stung with hope.

The amorphous chest under her hands hardened, and Carys blinked up into the face of a guardian, with arching horns and swooping wings. A whiplike tail lashed at her, and vicious claws sank into her sides. Carys screamed into the face of her kin, hating the dark facsimile and the Underhill for using it against her.

He roared back, fangs menacing, but—

Another caress on her nape, and then Carys felt his magick wrap around her, warm and silky, sinking inside. A tang of sweetness hit the back of her tongue, and the pain of her charred hands and battered chest faded away.

She touched the magick gently with her mind as it settled in her chest, a phantom weight just below her heart. It felt staid, good, safe, just like him.

Gavriel shuddered, the horns and wings sliding away like water over rock to reveal a fall of silvery hair. She caught him as his steaming body slumped, and she bore him as gently as she could to the ground.

The earth quaked beneath them and white strings of magick oozed from the air above the lake. Her ears rang with the Underhill's howl of rage.

Carys threw herself over him and covered them with her wings, as if she could hide him away from the Underhill. The hot puff of his breath rippled against the membranes, and Carys held still, listening desperately to his steady heartbeat.

Bursts of magick exploded over the lake, brighter than the moon, and the lake churned like a boiling cauldron. But nothing touched them on the shore, and as Carys held tight to her mate, the light slowly dimmed.

Finally, with a shudder that shook the mortal realm, the Underhill retreated.

The night faded once more into inky blue and soft darkness.

Only when the night creatures began to emerge from their dens and chitter to each other did Carys pull back her wings.

Gavriel lay beneath her on the pebbled beach, his eyes closed and face serene. His chest rose and fell evenly, and aside from the tears that made everything he wore but his boots unsalvageable, he looked untouched.

She blinked blearily down at him, her sleeping mate, and wondered . . . had she done it?

No voice in her head answered, but his magick fluttered happily in her chest.

She smiled, liking the feeling of him there.

Carys spread the cloak over them both before laying down beside him. With her head pillowed on her mate's chest and her arms filled with him, she let her eyes drift shut and the exhaustion take her, comforted to know, finally, she wouldn't wake alone.

Fourteen

Gavriel woke to a world so bright it stung his eyes. He blinked, not quite believing it was the sun warming his face.

An arm slid up his chest, the weight and warmth familiar even if he'd never woken in his mate's arms before, and he turned his head to behold his sleeping *cariad*.

Her face, tucked into the crook of his shoulder, was even softer in sleep, long lashes brushing her cheeks. He greedily studied all her precious features and elegant lines, all her colors and textures. Something about the contrast of her rosy pinks to his silvery opalescence pleased him deeply.

He followed where his eyes explored with his lips, finding her warm and lush. She smelled of evergreen and sunshine and just faintly of him. That pleased him, too.

Carys stirred in his arms as he kissed along her brow. As easily as breathing, her lips found his, a slow slide and warm suction. He nipped at her lips and chased her darting little tongue when it beckoned him inside.

It could've been moments or hours later when they finally pulled apart. Gavriel carded his fingers through the heavy mass of her hair, enthralled by her shiver when he ran a fingertip along a horn.

She cupped his face between her hands, and Gavriel wondered if she knew she held all of him in those little claws of hers.

"It's real," she whispered.

"Thanks to you."

She blushed prettily. "How do you feel?"

He took stock of himself, wiggling his toes and flexing his fingers. He remembered little after finishing his part of the ritual, but from the careful way she looked at him, he guessed the Underhill fought viciously to reclaim him.

"I'm perfect," he promised. "And I can feel it, my magick."

It burned inside him, like a little sun hidden behind his heart. Carys absently touched her breastbone, exactly where he felt it in his own chest, overflowing its former place.

"Do you feel it?"

"Yes," she said in wonder. "It's like . . . a friend, beating alongside my heart." And she guided his hand to her chest to feel it, a dual rhythm harmonizing just below her skin.

His heart clenched painfully with love. "You've given me everything, *cariad*. I swear to you, I will spend our days giving you everything in return." Even if it took a thousand years, he'd help free her kin and build a life worthy of her. It was the least she deserved.

"With your magick tethered to me, will I . . . ?"

"Yes. We fae aren't immortal, but we're long-lived. Will it trouble you, living so long?"

Her brow creased in a delicate frown. "I hadn't thought about it. I suppose it would if I outlived my family and clan, but . . ." She sighed and nuzzled into his chest. "I think I'll love my life with you, however long it may be."

"*Carys.*" He tipped up her chin to meet his kiss, humbled that one so sweet thought they could be happy with him. He'd make sure of it.

Gavriel had longed for centuries to feel the sun and wind on his face; he looked forward to diving in the lake and seeing the stars and smelling the richness of a forest. All that could wait—now, what he needed and wanted and longed for was his mate.

He deepened his kiss, tasting her moan as he swept his tongue inside to tangle with hers. He shifted above her, arms caging her in, and savored how she spread her legs to make room for him. He settled himself there, around his mate, everywhere he wanted to be.

"I ache for you," he told her between kisses down her throat. He kissed the hollow there, where her scent was strong, and couldn't resist tasting her, too. She gasped, hips shifting restlessly, as the flat of his tongue ran up her neck to her ear. "Are you ready, *cariad?* Or do you need more—?"

"I need *you*," she said, scraping her claws gently through his hair.

Gavriel swallowed hard, just keeping himself from falling on her like a mindless beast. This lovely creature awoke his lust as surely as his magick, both searing him from the inside out. He carefully undressed her with trembling hands, unwrapping the gift he'd been given. Once she was laid back on his cloak, naked and rosy, he was much less careful with his own scraps, tossing them somewhere so he could finally gorge on the sight of his mate.

Her heavy breasts with their dusky nipples quivered under his voracious gaze. Her wings curled around her slim shoulders, and her waist nipped in before flaring generously at her hips. And her legs . . . Gavriel had seen tragically little of her legs.

He took one small ankle in his hand to kiss the top of her foot, just above her talons. He ran his fingertips along the supple curve of her calf, up the soft thickness of her thigh, and down again. He longed to see the generous swells of her backside, no doubt perfect and plush just like the rest of her, but as much as the beast in him craved flipping her over to watch that backside bounce as he took her fast and hard, that had to wait.

Something about having her under him, open and giving, made

him painfully aware of how easily he could hurt her, small as she was compared to him. They would fit, he was her mate and made for her—but his cock looked almost monstrous as it lengthened and throbbed against her thigh.

He had to be slow. Gentle. Even if the thought of her squeezing him impossibly tight nearly made him spill.

"You're thinking very hard," she teased, though her eyes had gone shy.

"Just thinking of you," he said between kisses, "and everything I plan to do."

She hummed in pleasure. "Show me."

"Patience," he told her. And himself.

He lay down beside her and took her mouth again, already addicted to her taste. He let the heat build slowly, keeping his touches gentle, focusing on the unhurried drag of his lips and thumbs against her skin rather than the insistent throb of his greedy cock. It'd waited millennia for her, he'd last a few more moments.

She explored him too, running gentle fingers along his chest, his shoulders, then raked her claws down his back. The little points sank into his backside, and she rolled her hips, kissing the underside of his cock with her wet, molten core.

Gavriel shuddered and thrust against her once, twice, before clenching his teeth and reining himself back.

"I won't break," she said with an endearing huff. "I'm not made of glass."

"Oh, *cariad*, you're many things, but none of them that."

"What am I, then?" she said, pushing those perfect breasts at him, demanding.

He shuddered again, resolve cracking. He had good intentions, truly, but who was he to deny his mate?

"Where to begin?" He trailed his fingertips up her stomach. "First, you're exquisite." He watched her watch his finger delicately trace an impertinent nipple, begging for attention, and delighted in her sharp inhale. "And a perfect handful." She gasped when he took her breast in his hand and oh, he was right, the perfect size to fill his hands. He nearly lost himself in the plush give of them, watching his fingers sink into the warm softness.

She arched, pushing her breast further into his grip.

"What a lusty little wench you are," he chuckled, more delighted and aroused than he'd been in eons.

"What else?"

"You're kind and strong and so, so warm." He dragged his fingers down to her hips that undulated mindlessly. "You're unbreakable, Carys."

She stilled in surprise before tears gathered along her lashes, but he quickly kissed them away.

"No tears, love, not anymore." He took her mouth in a kiss deeper than the Underhill, needing her to feel the weight of his promise, his love, his heart.

"Do you know what else you are?" he asked while his fingers found and teased her core. Goddess, she burned, all slick heat in his hand.

She jerked her head from side to side, chasing the fingers he danced over her wet heat.

Gavriel kissed a trail from her mouth to her ear so she'd not just hear but feel it too when he said, "Mine. You're *mine*." And thrust two fingers inside her in one brutal move, making her arch and keen and scrape her little claws deliciously down his back. He relished the welts they'd leave, her mark, and set his fangs against her shoulder, not hard enough to bite but enough to leave his own mark.

She filled her little fist with his hair and pulled, arching as if to escape his ruthless pace, but he chased her down and added his thumb, circling her sensitive flesh as his long fingers curled inside her. Her back bowed, baring the column of her throat, and Gavriel kissed her there, feeling her cry of ecstasy against his lips.

He didn't slow even as she crested her first peak, and Carys moaned, protesting, "I can't, I can't."

"Of course you can," he promised.

Gavriel swallowed her cries this time, sinking his tongue into the hot well of her mouth. He'd never tire of this, the wet slide of his fingers inside her, the plush give of her lips, the drag of her nipples against his chest as she trembled and came apart beneath him. He devoured all of it greedily, male satisfaction thrumming through him to give his mate everything she wanted.

It would be his duty and his pleasure. Always.

Fifteen

Carys stared into the noonday sky, sated beyond being able to move. She'd pleasured and been pleasured before, either by a male of her clan or by her own hand, but none of it compared to the sure, wicked strokes of her mate's fingers.

I may not survive his cock.

Languid and replete, she turned her head to admire his fine form. He was nearly as tall as a guardian, with broad shoulders that tapered to a narrow waist and corded muscle packed onto a tight, lean frame. He exuded coiled strength, the sharp lines of his chest and abdomen stark against his opalescent skin, without being bulky like so many males of her kind. A sword rather than a battle-axe.

Gavriel rolled to his knees, leaving her bereft. She stared raptly as he clasped his hand, soaked in her slick, around his cock and pumped. The sight sent a quiver straight to her core. She'd thought she needed a moment, but watching him roughly handle that angry cock was too much temptation.

She waited for him to come to her with all that coiled strength and lust. She saw all the centuries he'd waited for his mate in the way he watched her, a predator waiting to pounce. Perhaps the intensity should've scared her, but the thought of him unleashed left her achy and clenching. She could take him and his lust—happily.

Unbreakable. That's what he'd called her. She felt like it then, stretching her arms above her head and arching her back just to see him devour her with his gaze. Under that hot stare, she wasn't useless or malformed. She'd survived the curse, the wilderness, the wildmen, the Underhill. She'd brought this fae warrior to his knees, and now she wanted all of him.

And he'd promised her everything she wanted.

When he still didn't come to her, eyes tight as he fought for control, Carys dipped her fingers into her wet heat, gathering more of her slick.

He grimaced and squeezed himself at the base. Carys rolled to her knees and reached for his cock, already weeping for her.

"I can do that for you," she purred, feeling exactly like the lusty wench he'd called her.

But Gavriel only grimaced and took her hand in his—to place at her side.

She couldn't help pouting.

"Oh, you can do that for me soon, love, and frequently, but it isn't your little hands I need right now."

Carys huffed and laid back again, thighs falling open. She adored how noble he was, but right then, she needed the ferocity his eyes promised.

"Then take what you need."

Letting out a groan that was more like a growl, Gavriel fell upon her, hungry lips nipping and sucking at her ear and neck. Carys hummed happily at the weight of him, loving how he fit into the cradle of her body.

"Do you know what you do to me, *cariad?* I try to be gentle, but I think you want me to fall on you and rut you like an animal."

"Yes yes yes . . ." she chanted as he teased the hot head of his cock through her folds.

"Hasn't anyone warned you to be careful what you wish for?" he said in that dark, lyrical purr she loved so much.

All she could manage was a needy moan because finally, finally he breached her, conquering his way inside—even when it became too much, even when she thought there was nothing more she could take. He kept a steady rhythm, pumping inside, working her until their hips flushed together, and Carys nearly choked at the fullness, the way he stretched her wide open and made room for himself.

She fluttered around him, stuffed full. She would've flown apart if it weren't for that cock pinning her to him, filling up all the empty places inside her.

Gavriel looked down to where their bodies joined, a wicked grin sliding across his face.

"Look at how well you take me." He retreated just a little, and Carys hissed at the emptiness he left behind. He crooned and hummed at her, sitting back on his heels to run his hands down her body and splay his big palms over her hips. His fingers dug into the giving flesh of her backside, and his thumbs spread her lips even wider.

She gasped when one ran over the slick seal of their bodies and nearly bucked off the ground when the second grazed her sensitive nub. Gavriel rumbled in pleasure, and she felt it, inside, along with her answering gush of heat. His grin turned insufferably smug. He pushed back inside with a delicious drag, his thumbs playing maddeningly with her sensitive flesh.

"Gavriel!" she keened.

"That's it, love. Give me your pleasure, then I'll take you like the beast you've made me."

She opened her mouth to protest, to tell him to come with her, but all that came out was a yelp as he ground his cock inside her and his thumb down on her nub all at once. Carys saw stars in the afternoon sky.

She'd barely come back to herself when he was there, pressed tight to her, his face looming just over hers. She canted her head for a kiss, and he gave it to her, their teeth clacking together as he hunted down her peak, hips thrusting like thunderclouds rolling down the mountain.

He clutched her to him in a punishing grip, making her meet him, making her take everything he gave. His eyes, hot as molten silver, trained on her breasts as they bounced. With a growl he dove to suck hard and bite lightly on a nipple.

Carys screamed and sobbed and scraped her claws through his silky hair, clutching tight, needing purchase. He released her with a wet pop then claimed the other.

It was too much, his pace, the tease of his hipbone against her nub with every thrust, his mouth at her breast. It was everything she wanted. On his next thrust, she seized in ecstasy, legs clamping tight around him, capturing him deep inside, just where she needed him.

Gavriel roared above her, teeth bared, fingers digging almost painfully into her backside. He heaved and pounded inside again, again, again and then a hot wash filled her, making her gasp with the fullness. Tremors racked her as his hips slowed to a soft rhythm but didn't quite stop.

He collapsed atop her, just catching himself on his elbow, and shook with the power of their release. She wiped away a trickle of sweat from his temple as they panted for breath. For the first time, he looked thoroughly mussed, and she couldn't help her own smug grin.

When he saw it, he twitched inside her, and Carys raised a brow.

"Oh, *cariad*," he said in a voice a little deeper and more dangerous than before, his eyes glittering and sharp as diamonds, "I'm far from done with you."

In a move so quick only a fae could do it, he pulled out and flipped her over. He groaned appreciatively and sank his fingers into her backside, kneading the generous flesh. Being on her belly sparked a fresh wave of lust, and Carys pulled her trembling knees under her, slick trickling down her thighs.

A dark chuckle thrummed from his chest, and he gave her backside a light love tap. Carys gasped when his fingers slid through her wetness then speared inside. It was different than before, his fingers somehow larger and deeper.

Carys moaned and wiggled her hips, wanting more.

His chuckle turned into a groan. "You do it on purpose, drive me to insanity," he said, and then his cock was replacing his fingers, gliding through the hot syrup she'd made. "Goddess." He pushed her knees wider and filled his hands with her hips, making her meet his every stroke as he pumped inside. If his fingers had felt bigger and deeper, it was nothing to his cock. He hit somewhere inside her Carys couldn't name, hadn't known existed, and it made her toes curl and wings flutter.

"Look at your pretty wings," he crooned. He kneaded the wing base while his other hand sought her nub and traced maddening little circles.

Carys arched, wings splayed, and thrust mindlessly back to meet him.

"Almost, love," he rumbled, and then his arms were around her, pulling her up. He sat her on his lap, impaled on him, and drew her knees apart with his thighs, wider than she thought possible. Carys reached back to sink her hands in his hair and gasped when his closed around her breasts.

Gavriel ran the tip of his nose along the curve from her shoulder to neck before setting his teeth there and thrusting hard enough to make her keen. She bounced wildly on him as his rhythm broke down and his grip grew punishing. He snarled into her shoulder, pounding once, twice before crushing her to his chest and sealing them together. A hot wash flooded her, filling her to the brim.

Carys came apart on a cry. Her wings fluttered and her tail wrapped around his thigh, holding on tight, with everything she was.

She wouldn't take this moment or any other with him for granted.

She was the last of her kind, their only hope of survival, but in that moment, all she was, all she wanted to be, was Gavriel's.

A long time later, after they managed to get into her little shelter and debauch her nest of blankets, Carys indulged in a luxurious stretch, her limbs heavy with the aftermath of so much pleasure. She loved the feel of her skin sliding against his, loved too how his body moved with hers to keep as much contact as possible.

She did it again, it felt so good.

A tired rumble reverberated against her back and wings, and the hand that had been lazily tracing patterns between her breasts splayed to press her more firmly against his chest.

Gavriel nuzzled then nipped her ear before muttering, "I'm a fae warrior, nigh immortal, and if you keep that up, I'll keep you here, bound to this bower for the next hundred years."

So she had to do it again, teasing her backside on the hot length of him. "Do you promise?"

"Insatiable wench," he accused, wrapping a hand around her thigh to pull it over his. He held her like that, open and ready, and pushed inside, rolling his hips so that on each maddeningly slow stroke, he reached just a little deeper. He held her head in his other palm, claiming her mouth for a kiss that was just as slow and deep.

It was soft this time, languid lovemaking that crested like the dawn, steadily until the sky filled with light. Carys bit her lip around a smile as she came, feeling his contented sigh flutter the hair at her temple. He kissed her there as they settled again into a tangled puddle of limbs.

Gavriel lazily ran his fingers up and down the thigh he'd draped over his, making no move to pull away, his softening cock still buried deep. His hand strayed along her leg, up to her lower belly, where he traced the faint shape of himself inside her. Carys moaned at the sensation, finding she loved the feel of him like this, holding him close in all ways.

Finally his hand came to rest on her belly, splayed wide to keep her tucked against his big body. She nearly dozed, content and warm and surrounded by her mate.

This was everything she'd hoped it would be; there would be challenges, of course there would, but there would also be time to learn each other, face the challenges together, perhaps even—

"Gavriel!" Carys gasped, eyes flying wide, and she clutched the hand at her stomach.

Quicker than she could see, Gavriel rolled her under him, his lips pulled back in a snarl. The breath whooshed from her lungs as her wings were crushed between them.

"What is it?" he growled, searching for a threat.

"Nothing, nothing," she soothed, petting his forearm until he finally laid back.

His eyes were still wary as she rolled to face him.

She licked her lips, mouth dry when she said, "You and I . . . only mates can have fledglings for my kind."

We could have made one already.

Happiness suffused his features, making her chest clench with nerves.

"I hope we do," he said. "A child of you and I, it'd be a blessing."

"You want children?"

His expression went carefully neutral. "Very much. Do you?"

Carys swallowed on a dry throat. "Would you hate me if I said no? At least, not yet?"

"I could never hate you, *cariad*, especially not for that." Rising up on an elbow, Gavriel's gaze was tender as he smoothed back her hair. "My magick can ensure my seed doesn't take until you're ready, *fy annwyl*. But a child, *our* child would be a gift—no matter the size of their wings or if they had none at all." She flushed, realizing he knew her deepest fears about mothering a fledgling. He kissed her forehead, murmuring, "But I already have everything I need. You are my world, Carys. I meant it when I promised you everything, even if it's time."

Carys threw her arms around him, unable to voice everything she felt. So she showed him in kisses, claiming his mouth, his throat, his chest, his cock with her lips. She played with him for as long as he could stand, then went eagerly when his patience ran out and he pulled her up his body.

"Does the block affect anything else?" she asked, straddling his hips as his hungry gaze followed her swaying breasts.

He kneaded her thighs impatiently as she took him in hand and sank down. "Of course not," he rumbled. "You question if I can still satisfy my mate, make her scream and beg for me?"

"Never never never," she cried, setting her hands on his chest, feeling his heart thunder under her palms. She rolled her hips to meet his every thrust, claiming him as fiercely as he did her, this fierce fae warrior who was so, so good and gentle with her.

Her heart still bled for her kin, and she was as determined to free them. Soon they'd return to the glen and keep those who'd been turned to stone safe until the curse could be broken. She'd carry their traditions and stories with her, keeping those safe, too. But today, tonight, tomorrow were for her and Gavriel, for beginnings, for healing.

Soon enough they'd face the Underhill and the curse. For now, it was enough to be in her mate's arms, to give him her love, and to let him show her what it meant to be *cariad*.

Part 2

I

658 AD
Caer Gwyn, deep in Eryri

The soft roar of the falls near their home was a soothing rumble, and Carys let it ease the worst of her nerves as she tied the last leather strap of Gavriel's vambrace. When she stepped back to look at her work, she found a fae warrior standing before her.

Resplendent in his armor, the metal gleamed blue in the morning light. The plates curved with his form, as if liquid metal had been poured over and molded to his frame. It was almost a shame that no one else would see it under his glamour. He'd made the armor himself over the years, piece by piece, all in his forge during the long, dark winter days. Carys could hardly imagine a whole army of such fearsome warriors and understood better how his people had dominated the realms for so long.

She ran a hand down the smooth plate of his cuirass, glad at least that while no one would see it, it was there nevertheless. Though not imbued with magick like his former armor, forged in the fires of Faerie eons ago, it was still much better than the mail shirts and boiled leather all the other warriors wore. It kept him safe.

"Are you sure you must go?" she asked, not for the first time. She cringed as she said it, hearing the plaintive tone in her voice, but the words escaped her lips.

Gavriel grinned patiently. "King Cynddylan wishes to speak of next season's plans. The Northumbrian king won't be content and we must convince Cadwaladr and Gwynedd of this or else Powys will be vulnerable."

Carys made a noncommittal sound, fiddling with the ties she'd already knotted. She admired how Gavriel had thrown himself into adopting Albion as his new home. In the eighty mortal years since freeing Gavriel of the Underhill, the Pritani tribes she'd known as a girl had collapsed and reformed, known now as the Cymry, but to the Saxons circling like vultures to the east, they were the Welsh.

Deep in the windswept region of Eryri, they'd made their home by a dense copse of trees. A small lake lapped nearby, fed by a waterfall that gushed in the winter and trickled in the summer. As they built their home at Caer Gwyn, the land Carys had once known grew and changed around her.

New kingdoms arose, with kings rather than chieftains who built great stone caers to guard against the waves of Saxon attacks from the east. As the kingdoms of Gwynedd, Powys, Pengwern, Dyfed, and Gwent grew, so too did Gavriel's interest. Though their lands were nominally claimed by Gwynedd, Gavriel travelled to all the courts, making friends with the kings and lending his aid.

All the kings knew of Caer Gwyn and believed Gavriel a descendant of the nobleman who built the great caer. In truth, it was always Gavriel, his glamour fooling the human eyes to think him someone new.

The past decades, Gavriel's commitment had grown with the Cymry finding some success, lands retaken from their Northumbrian and Mercian enemies to the east. A buzz of excitement ran through Albion itself, a sense of hope the Cymry hadn't had in many years. With the successes, it sometimes felt as though he was always off with one court or another, fighting to regain lost Cymry territory, more than he was with her.

She couldn't begrudge him wanting to see more of this world. Trapped for so long, he was anxious to roam and experience everything he could. He'd been so patient with her in those first years together, finding a place to make their home. He built her a strong home of stone, reinforced with his magick, and now their roots ran deep into the land. She'd rarely strayed from Caer Gwyn since, as their home grew over the years and had everything she needed.

But *he* needed more.

He caught her fidgeting fingers and raised them to his lips, kissing each one with a patient smile.

It wasn't fair, truly, how dashing and dangerous he looked in his armor and smiling at her like that. The blush rose to turn her even pinker, and she couldn't help the grin twitching across her lips.

Eighty mortal years and he still made her blush.

"I won't be long," he promised, "it's just to Pengwern to hear Cynddylan's plan. His army is wintering there—it will be safe." He answered her unspoken question.

It was silly of her to worry over him, really. A fae warrior as seasoned as he, with the full might of his magick, nothing human could truly harm him. He was faster than their arrows, stronger than their war machines. His armor would keep him from the worst a human male could do, and he healed nearly as fast they could wound him.

What's more, with his magick, he could bend Albion around him. So long as he'd been to a place before, he could transport himself there again in little time, from anywhere. He came home to her at night when he could, even while he was away, so long as he wouldn't be missed. With any luck, this meeting would run short and he could return to her before she'd begun supper.

She knew all this, but it was never easy to let him leave her.

Perhaps she should go with him, if it would be just a meeting and safe . . . but . . .

She didn't want to leave Caer Gwyn and all the precious things they guarded here.

Still, "I miss you, is all." She wouldn't ask him not to go, not when fighting alongside the Cymry meant so much to him. He'd been great friends with Cadwallon ap Cadfan, King of Gwynedd, before his death, and was still good friends with his son, Cadwaladr, even if the son was more reluctant to fight. But she knew from his stories that he liked travelling east to Pengwern best and had felt a kinship to its king, Cynddylan, since the man was a boy. They were brothers in arms, a bond Carys couldn't offer him, one she thought his soul needed after the horrors of losing Faerie.

That smile of his turned devilish, one side kicked up higher than the other, and a familiar heat sparked low in her belly. She knew that look well.

"Have I been neglectful, *cariad?*" he asked, kissing her palm, then the inside of her wrist. "Do you miss my touch when I'm gone?"

"I miss everything," she said, voice gone husky. She watched, entranced, as he kissed up her arm to the sleeve of her shift.

He traced the embroidered pattern at the hem, raising gooseflesh on her arms.

"Do you think of me while I'm away? Do you imagine I'm here with you, even when I'm miles away?"

He stepped forward and she retreated a step in turn. His quicksilver eyes flashed, and she saw that predatory part of him that lived inside, the one that liked to chase her through their little forest and ply her with kisses as he crooned the word *mine* into her skin.

Gavriel crowded her toward their large bed, rumpled still from their slumber. She felt the soft resistance of the blankets hit her backside and stopped.

"Do you imagine your fingers are mine as you pleasure yourself?"

Her breath hitched. Making love had grown into a daily ritual for them, a pleasurable way to connect and reaffirm their bond. When he left her for days at a time, the cravings of her body often grew too much to bear.

"Yes," she whispered.

"Because you know it's mine. Your body, your release, your pleasure—they're mine, even in your mind." He took up all her vision, looming over her like a warrior from legend. "And when the nights grow long and lonely and I'm kept away from you, I fist my cock to the thought of you in our bed, pleasuring yourself to thoughts of me."

A finger traced the neckline of her shift, teasing the warm tops of her breasts as her breathing quickened. His eyes strayed down to watch, and she may have breathed deeper than necessary, just to make them rise and fall more dramatically. Eighty years and he was still enchanted with her breasts. She found it endearing.

"Many peoples consider it lucky for a warrior to bed his woman before battle," he rumbled. He closed the little space between them, crushing her breasts against the unyielding plane of his armor and capturing her in his arms. His hands found their way to her backside, where he kneaded and squeezed, urging her up onto her tip-talons.

"But you're not going to battle," she reminded him between fervent kisses.

Another rumble from deep in his chest that had her wings fluttering in pleasure. "No, but it still couldn't hurt."

Her whole body flushed a deeper pink. She could never resist him, not truly, but, "We just finished your—"

Quicker than her eyes could see, he pulled the wide neck of her shift from her shoulders, careful not to tangle it in her wings. It puddled at her feet, baring her to the cool morning air in their bedchamber.

"Oh," she sighed, talons leaving the ground as he picked her up and set her at the center of their bed. Her legs fell open and he was there, finding his place between them, exactly where he belonged.

The cold metal of his armor almost burned as she wrapped her legs around him, and she hissed at the delicious contrast of it to the burning heat of his mouth as he kissed a path down her body.

She shivered when he pressed hot kisses to her soft belly and mons.

"Do you need something to remember me by?" he asked before his tongue flicked against her sensitive flesh.

Her back bowed and she dug her claws into his long white-blonde hair, loosening the braids she'd plaited to keep it out of his face. He moved above her, arranging her just as he wanted. With a leg thrown over his shoulder and the other crooked back to her hip, she lay prone before him. And he feasted.

Skin gleaming opalescent in the brightening daylight, he pinned her there, to their bed, for—she didn't know how long. *Too long.* Her wings fluttered, the only part of her able to move as he used his weight to keep her still and receive his attentions.

She toyed with her breasts as his tongue speared inside, and when it finally grew too much to bear, she snuck a hand down her mons to press where she needed it and where he neglected on purpose. With two strokes she was nearly flying, but a growl rumbled from him that had her clutching at his tongue.

"You know that's mine," he scolded, laving his tongue across her once more before straightening. She whimpered, bereft, and had to bite down on a hiss when one of his fingers began to trace her slit up and down, up and down, but never deep, never enough.

"Good mates let their males take care of them."

"Good males let their mates come," she growled.

A wicked smile danced across his face. "Oh, I intend to let you, *cariad.* Just not quite yet. Will you be a good mate for me?"

She rolled her hips, trying to guide his fingers where she needed them, but he knew her game and moved his hand away.

Carys would have grumbled again but instead watched, rapt, as he leaned over her, planting a hand beside her in the bed, and used the other to unlace his braies.

Still clothed and armored head to toe, a few loose laces allowed his cock to jut free. Already thick and arching for her, a pearlescent bead crowned the tip. If they'd been newly mated, she might have missed how he trembled just slightly, and she grinned to herself to know he was near his own break. But his game was too delicious, and if it kept him with her a little longer, she was happy to play.

Fisting himself at the root, he teased his cockhead over her soaked slit in decadent, slow drags. The sight of him, his cock slightly darker than the rest of his grayish opalescence, armored and armed against her flushed bare skin, made her shudder in delight. She buried her claws in the blankets and grit her fangs, determined to let him wring every morsel of pleasure from her.

He circled her nub, driving her nearly mad, once, twice, then tapped it with the underside of his cock. She almost bucked but held still, shoulders and breasts quivering with the effort.

"Good mate," he rumbled, pleased.

"Good mate," she agreed, then arched just a little, drawing his gaze to her aching nipples. She was past subtly.

"Ah, *cariad*," he breathed. His cock slid home just as his warm mouth closed around her breast. She cried out in ecstasy at the dual sensations, and he set himself a brutal rhythm, her other breast bouncing against his cheek.

He released her nipple with a wet pop and descended on the other. She buried a hand in his hair for something to hold onto and pinched her freed breast, needing the pressure.

A hand slid under her, and his fingers dug into the ample flesh of her backside. He angled her just so, driving deeper and longer and harder and—

Carys gasped, flying apart as he pounded inside, not stopping even as she crested and came down. It wasn't until he'd pushed her up the peak again that he roared, filling her up and pulling her down again with him.

Crushed under his weight and armor, Carys panted for breath, her legs shaking with the force of her pleasure.

After a moment, he lifted just enough to kiss between her breasts and then up her neck, to her ear, where he rumbled, "Again."

Her lips fell open in surprise, letting out a gasp of delight when he rolled her to her front. Carys moaned as he pushed her knees apart and filled his hands with her wide hips, pulling her back to him, their flesh meeting in a wet smack.

"Gavriel . . ." she pleaded.

"You cannot miss me too much if you still feel me for days."

She lay there long after he was gone and the sun had begun its trek across the sky. If she didn't rise, it almost felt as though he hadn't left. His scent still clung to their bed, and when she closed her eyes, she could imagine him there, just behind her, dozing late into the morning like they sometimes did when they began their day with lovemaking.

It was the animals' loud complaints that finally got her up and dressed.

Knotting her apron around her waist, Carys was greeted outside by a warm shaft of sunlight and many agitated bleats and brays.

"All right, all right, don't get your tails in a twist," she laughed, wagging her finger at the goats.

The goats and donkeys, too, followed her around the paddock fence as she gathered their breakfast. When they were all happily gobbling away, she laid seed for the chickens, hay for the ponies, and went with the dogs out to the eastern field to move the sheep to the lower meadow.

The sun held for her morning tasks, the sky politely waiting to rain until she was back inside. She grumbled as the dogs shook off the mud and damp on her clean stone floors, but it only took a few wide eyes and apologetic licks to earn ear scratches.

They followed her about the large home as she did her afternoon chores, keeping her quiet company. Her kind hadn't often kept animals, but Carys adopted the practice a few years after settling at Caer Gwyn. She enjoyed their gentleness and antics, and the milk, wool, and eggs they provided made it simple to remain at the caer. When they had too much of something, which was often, Gavriel would take it into one of the nearest villages.

She was content to stay behind with the animals and watch over them and their home.

Perhaps it was unnecessary and even foolish of her, but the idea of leaving Caer Gwyn for long made dread pool in her belly. They had everything they needed here.

And more importantly, what was left of her people was here, tucked away and safe.

They had returned to the cliffs near Caerdyf for a brief time to collect all the things Carys had hidden away, the sentimental things she hadn't taken with her in her flight north. Yet they hadn't lingered, hadn't chosen a home near the old, empty clanhomes nor the Pritani tribe that first wrought her kind.

So they wandered north again, finding a secluded place deep within Eryri. They were alone out here, surrounded by the mountains and a glen of windswept trees. A small waterfall splashed into the lake that lapped near their front door. Over the years, their home had grown into a sprawling stone structure, accommodating all their needs and interests. She'd planted gardens around the home, vegetables and berries and herbs and daffodils. Mats of ivy clung to the western walls, and her rose bushes had grown hearty over the last twenty years.

A spacious bedchamber, large kitchen and larder, library, great room, two solars, and chambers for all the things they found and kept and made through the decades completed the main house. Gavriel had his forge outside and he'd built her a dovecote as well. And to the south, another structure, another bedchamber of sorts.

Perhaps crypt was more apt, but she tried not to think like that. Instead, she thought of it as a mausoleum—a longer, fancier word for the same thing maybe, but to her, it made it sound as though her kin were merely asleep.

It was silly, but Carys insisted they add windows to the building where her kin were kept. The two dozen stone statues they'd recovered stood timeless, protected from the elements, but something drove her to make sure they had sunlight and a view. She didn't know how much of them was left inside those stone husks, but if there was a chance they could see or hear or feel, she wanted them at least to have a bit of sun.

Alone as she was, her kin beckoned her into the mausoleum once the rain abated. She left the dogs at the door to enter the eerily quiet room. The low light of late afternoon cast long shadows over her kin.

She wended around the stone shells, touching their arms and faces.

Of those here, she knew only one by name. Frey. An intense, broody male who fought quicker than he thought. They'd been of a similar age, so long ago, and despite wishing so desperately for a mate, she'd always been relieved it wasn't him.

Still, a familiar face was an odd comfort.

All the faces had grown familiar over the decades, and she hated that she didn't know or remember their names. Perhaps once she'd known them; there had never been many guardians, a few hundred perhaps, with their numbers dwindling as the Green Isle was overrun with invaders and the Pritani either slain or driven away. Perhaps she would have recognized them with a little warmth in their cheeks and life in their eyes.

Carys didn't know how many guardians had been slaughtered that awful night and how many were rendered stone by Titania's curse. Like a coward, she'd run from the glen instead of keeping them safe.

Gavriel had told her many times there was nothing she could have done, and over the years she'd come to believe him. Yet it didn't stop her from regretting leaving them there, alone, defenseless.

She should have burned the dead, said the proper rites.

By the time she and Gavriel returned, what was left of the guardians were hunks of desiccated flesh clinging by moldering tendons to bone bleached white from the sun. Gavriel had been the one to move the remains. She made the funeral pyres, stripped the wood with her bare hands, and had lit the flames when it was time, but she couldn't bear looking upon the rotted corpses.

Only a handful of statues had been left in the glen. They found a few more in the surrounding forest. And three they recovered from nearby villages that had taken the statues to guard their gates. From these humans she and Gavriel learned that, days after it happened, the surviving Pritani had braved the glen. Seeing the massacre, they carried off the statues they could and never returned. Other curious humans had come and claimed more, leaving only those few for Carys and Gavriel to find.

Scattered to the winds, she had no idea how to find her remaining kin. They had come across a few more in their wanderings before settling at Caer Gwyn, but the twenty now sheltered here couldn't be the last of her kind. She didn't accept that.

Yet . . . she didn't know what else to do.

Gavriel hadn't come across more in his travels to the Cymry courts. And they were no closer to finding an answer to the curse, nor where Morrígan could be or how to free the fae of the Underhill.

So many years, and so little to show for it.

Your answers aren't here at Caer Gwyn.

No, they weren't. But she . . . she didn't have the courage yet to seek them out past her borders.

With a sigh and heavy heart, she changed the sprig of lavender she left for the guardians with a fresh one and returned to the main house.

Her supper was a lonely one yet again, and she barely tasted the stew she reheated over the kitchen fire. She stayed awake long after the moon had crested, keeping Gavriel's supper warm.

It was only when the candle had burned to a stub and the dogs whuffed at her that Carys finally rose from her stool and retreated to the bedchamber.

Retrieving her shift from the floor, she pulled it over her shoulders.

She had others, but that he'd touched it that morning, that he'd held her against him the night before while she wore it . . .

Crawling into bed, she let the dogs sleep at her feet, finding comfort in their warm bodies and steady breathing. They were calm and content, and she tried to be so, too. Even if her worries, unnecessary and unformed as they were, only allowed her fitful rest.

Gavriel slipped through the shadows into their bedchamber, the magick winking out around him to reveal a quiet scene. The barest light eked in from the windows, dawn threatening to chase away the night. A banked fire glowed in the hearth. Two heads rose curiously from the bed, and the dogs quietly leapt down to patter to him.

They stopped and whined, sitting on their haunches with worry widening their eyes.

Blood dripped onto the wood floor.

He opened his mouth to . . . he didn't know. Words clogged in his throat as he watched the sleeping form of his *cariad*, quiet in her rest.

He didn't want to wake her. He didn't want her to see him like this.

She was too soft, too good after everything he'd seen this day. He needed her goodness and softness more than anything then, but he couldn't form the words.

But he needed . . .

Whether it was the dogs' unhappy sounds or the dripping blood puddling on the floor, something woke her.

He heard her intake of breath, watched her roll to his side of their bed. He yearned for her to open her eyes—and dreaded it, too. Her eyes flickered open, the gold of coins and crowns in the low light. Her gaze focused on him immediately, and she gasped, blankets thrown back in a flurry of wings and golden hair.

"Gavriel!"

She rushed to his side, her claws so gentle as she took his face between her hands. The warm clasp of them, the slight rasp of calluses, nearly broke him.

"What's happened?" she demanded, the gold coins of her eyes rimmed in white.

His lips peeled back in a pained grimace. "It's gone."

"What's gone?"

"Everything. Pengwern. The Saxons, they attacked without warning. We weren't ready—and the fire—"

She caught him as his knees buckled, easing his fall. Slumped on his knees, he clung to her, and she embraced him without hesitation, soaking her shift in blood to hold his head and wrap him up in her wings. Gavriel wept into the softness of her shoulder, the brush of her hair and sweetness of her scent rending his heart into even smaller tatters.

For all his strength, for all his magick, he couldn't stop it. He could heal himself and his mate, too. Could disguise them to trick the human eye. Could move boulders and trees and earth, even fold the realm around him to move miles in one step. He could concentrate his magick into a nearly physical thing, had used it to pleasure his mate and stun enemies on the battlefield. He could use it to condense fire, raise water, and coax plants to grow quicker.

All this his magick could do—and yet he'd been powerless to stop the slaughter.

Carys didn't try to soothe him with platitudes, but hummed a lullaby to him. He barely heard over his tears, but the vibrations thrummed through him from head to toe.

After a long while, he shuddered, tears spent.

He held still when she set him back to look over. Eyes sad and full of sympathy, she began to unlace his armor. Piece by piece, she set the plates aside, piling them neatly. He heard her relieved sigh to discover not much of the blood was his and what wounds he'd received had already scabbed over.

When he was down to his shirt and braies, she drew him a bath in their large wooden tub. The part of his magick that now lived inside her helped make quick work of heating enough water; all she had to do was swirl a finger over the surface and faint wisps sank into the water. Steam soon rose from the surface invitingly.

The burn of it nearly made him hiss, nearly drew him from the horrified numbness that had claimed him as he transported himself from the wreckage of Pengwern back to Caer Gwyn. But it was his mate, soft and gentle and compassionate, who finally called him back home.

She ran a cloth over every inch, cleansing him of the horrors. Working him into a trance as she circled the tub, she was never not touching him, her hands or tail running in reassuring patterns across his skin.

Under her sweet ministrations, he was able to speak of what had happened. How he'd arrived early for the meeting to speak with Cynddylan. How the king's chiefs had all arrived by noonday. Barely had their talks begun when the alarm was raised. A Saxon force of thousands descended on Pengwern, catching the Cymry unprepared. The great hall was set ablaze, every home raided, every man and woman slaughtered.

Cynddylan had fallen protecting his sisters.

The fire consumed everything so quickly, and through the blaze and carnage, Gavriel could only save little Princess Heledd, the youngest of Cynddylan's sisters. With a handful of survivors, he led them west. The princess's cries still rang in his ears, her screams for forgiveness, that it was all her fault, she'd told her brother she hated him for scolding her the day before. Gavriel had soothed her, but the girl wouldn't be consoled. The fire that claimed her home and family burned in her eyes long after Gavriel brought her and the few others to neighboring Powys and safety.

"It's gone," he said, voice raw from the smoke and screams. "Pengwern is nothing now and the Saxons will divide the land between them. All the gains . . . all those lives, gone. Cynddylan . . ."

"Shh," Carys soothed, carding her fingers and lavender-scented soap through his hair.

Gavriel didn't want to, but the battle spilled out of him, every horrible detail he'd witnessed. Once, eons ago, he was a fae warrior and general to his Queen Rhiannon, but that was in another life. It was easy to forget how fleeting human life could be, how easily they destroyed one another. He'd allowed himself to care too much for them, hadn't been able to save them, just like . . .

Carys kissed his eyelids closed and used the corner of the cloth to wash his face, gentle as butterfly wings. With strong thumbs she massaged his palms and fingers, up his forearms to his shoulders. Firm fingers and gently scraping claws worked his neck, and he let his head fall back onto the pillows of her breasts, words and tears and soul spent.

"I know, *fy nghariad*," she whispered to him, and wrapped her arms around him, holding him together with her words and arms and goodness. "I know."

He hadn't thought he could sleep after witnessing so much bloodshed again, but with the warmth of his cariad wrapped around him, his head tucked to her chest so he could hear her every strong heartbeat and the slight hum of his magick just behind it, he managed.

She held him long into the morning, through fitful sleep and night-terrors. He awoke thinking he'd find Cynddylan's blood on his hands as he held his friend's innards inside his ruined chest. There'd been no time for last words, no breath left in Cynddylan's wet lungs to swear him to vengeance or to protect his sisters. From one moment to the next, his friend's eyes went dark and his chest didn't rise again.

When Gavriel opened his eyes, though, it was to find the beautiful sight of his mate, all her blushing pinks and sunshine golds on display in the bright daylight. He watched her under heavy lids as she cleaned his armor, little pink tongue stuck between her teeth as she meticulously wiped away every trace of blood and gore.

He dozed to her soft sounds and next woke when she drew his hair away from his face and urged food down his throat. He didn't want food, the anguish turning his stomach, but she coaxed him sweetly with promises. When the food was mostly gone and the dogs happily filled their bellies with the rest, she slid naked into their bed beside him.

Skin to skin, he soaked in her comfort. She offered it like she did everything, openly and without reservation.

His heart bled for his friends and what this meant for the land he'd come to love, but already, his mate had begun to heal him in ways only she could.

Running his nose along the part of her wild hair, he kissed her forehead. "I love you, *cariad*," he murmured.

It took many months for him to shed the last shards of his grief. Perhaps that was quick, perhaps it was slow—fae moved and lived according to their own, much longer times. He ventured only to the nearby villages, and, even then, it felt like too far from his mate.

The only news was dire, that Powys was now the eastern edge of Cymru, that Northumbria and Mercia had grown bold in raiding the borders. The danger was still far away from the villages near Caer Gwyn, but the horror of it was close in Gavriel's heart. He couldn't bear going to the villages after a time.

Instead, he stayed with Carys at their home. He came to understand why she liked the animals so well. There was something calming in their nature; they could be wild and unpredictable, even ornery and violent, but they were true.

He tended their animals and worked their land alongside his mate, and he was content.

Human affairs carried only heartache. He had a home, he had a good life—and most importantly, he had a mate whose smiles he lived for. Carys filled all the sore, aching parts of him with her light, and he often found himself following her around their lands like her loyal dogs, just to be near her.

He couldn't save the Cymry. He was but one fae, with a mate to protect and care for.

Both of their peoples were still languishing under curses. It was time he devoted himself to them. He owed it to their people and to his mate, too.

II

"Excellent, just like that. One more push for me."

The woman clutching Carys's shoulder bore down with one last tired wail, and in the next moment, Carys's hands were full of warm, wet, screaming child. Carys crooned to the little boy, showing him off to his mother, Alys. Even though her legs trembled and she'd still the afterbirth to go, Alys smiled down at her new baby, besotted.

Taking care of the cord and the afterbirth when it came, Carys cleaned up Alys and her baby boy, bustling them into bed and tidying up the cottage with a practiced hand. This wasn't her first baby—it wasn't even her hundredth. Carys had helped bring Alys into the world almost six-and-twenty years ago now, and she'd come screaming just like her boy did.

Carys couldn't tell her that, of course. Not when the glamour Gavriel's magick afforded her made the humans see a young midwife nary older than Alys.

It'd taken a long time to get used to, and Carys wasn't sure she even was yet, taking in her appearance in a looking glass and seeing no real signs of the centuries she'd lived. She'd watched Alys's mother Elin, and her mother, and her mother before that, all grow from girls to women to mothers. She had vague memories of how her kind had once aged, how their manes went gray and deep lines fanned from their eyes. She had none of it in her own face, even if she often felt every year she'd lived inside.

Gavriel had always been this way and didn't quite understand her struggle, though he tried to. Mortal time was nearly meaningless to a being as long-lived and powerful as a fae, and Carys saw this in the way he rarely hurried or rushed. When he set himself a task or discovered a new craft, he devoted himself to it for days, years even. There was no sense of wasting time, as time wasn't something a fae could waste.

The mindset gave her peace sometimes—it allowed her to slow down, to appreciate all the beauties of her world. It also gave her ample time to explore her own interests and crafts.

In the last centuries, Carys hadn't ventured far from Caer Gwyn, but she did enjoy coming the village of Harlech when there was a need. Rediscovering the learning she'd gotten from the druid healers all those years ago gave her visiting pleasure, and she'd set herself the goal two-hundred years past to learn to read and write. Gavriel spoiled her with books, most of them on healing and plants, using a little of the wealth they'd found in gold veins crisscrossing their lands.

Gavriel didn't know if it was because he was fae or because of his time in the Underhill that he had such an affinity for finding precious things in the ground. Whatever it was, it helped them build a comfortable life at Caer Gwyn and supported them through the centuries.

Upon learning to read and write, she'd taken to writing down her own notes from what she remembered of her teachings, as well as the wisdom of other healers she spoke with. Sharing that knowledge and easing the burdens of mortal women renewed a sense of purpose inside her, one that had floundered as she and Gavriel spent fruitless years trying to find a way to free their peoples without any luck.

It could be difficult to retain their urgency and cause when the years slipped past without any real success. They'd found a handful more of her stone-bound kin, and Gavriel had taken to collecting books and manuscripts of human legends and stories of his people. But otherwise, there was no progress, no hint of the Underhill, no word from his Queen Rhiannon, no sign of her sister Morrígan.

Just . . . nothing.

When she grew too despondent over it, she came to the village.

Surrounded by humans and mortality, the reminder of the life still living throughout Albion renewed her spirits.

Setting a cup of water near Alys, she brushed the woman's hair for her and plaited it.

"He's perfect," Alys whispered, counting all the baby's fingers and toes. It was her firstborn after several early miscarriages that, with proper medicines and a serious if uncomfortable talk with Alys and her husband Owain, had thankfully not repeated.

"He is," Carys agreed, heart glowing at the sight.

This could be your joy, too.

She grit her teeth and fluffed Alys's pillow. It wasn't her time yet, not when they were no closer to saving their people. To bring a child into the world, where they would have no playmates, no kin . . .

Carys cleared her throat. "Time to show him off," she said.

Alys grabbed her hand before she could fetch Owain.

"Thank you, for everything." Alys's eyes shone with her happiness, and Carys smiled back, heart full.

It's enough.

"Don't think of it, *fy ffrind*," she soothed.

Leaving Alys comfortable in her bed, Carys went to the front of the cottage and opened the door. Outside, a small crowd had gathered, a nervous Owain at their head. He swung to face the open door, worry carving stark lines beneath his eyes.

"And—?"

"Mother and child are well," Carys hurried to assure him. "You can see them."

With a relieved sigh, Owain hustled inside.

Carys held up a hand when a few others went to follow. "Just the father for now. Let him meet his son."

Through the crowd, a bald head pushed through bodies until a sour, scowling face stood before her. "Out of the way, *gwiddon*," spat Arnall, the local priest and Carys's latest foe. For as long as she'd been coming to Harlech to offer her skills, she'd had one saintly man or another heckling at her heels. She usually didn't pay them or their insults much heed, but Arnall's venom was particularly potent.

She'd lamented the passing of the old ways and old religions—the adoption of the churches and priests seemed yet another death knell to the people and beliefs once native to Albion. But the new ways and new religion had dug deep roots, and all she could do was keep the old ways alive within herself and use the old knowledge when it could help.

Most of the Cymry hadn't totally forgotten the old ways; their folklore and stories and traditions were still full of vestiges of the Pritani that had created her kind and fought so hard to keep their island. Most folk welcomed her and her knowledge, and she wasn't the only healer to practice the old ways in Harlech. But like a moth to a flame, practitioners of Arnall's ilk naysaid and spat untruths about her.

And what was worse, vehement in his faith, he baptized babes in the nearby river rather than the village church, claiming if St. John had done it, so too would they. More than one child had caught their death from the cold water.

"Give them a moment's peace, *offeiriad*. The boy is healthy and strong and can see you tomorrow."

Arnall's thin lips pursed. He'd never liked Carys or Alys or any woman, really.

"There isn't a moment to lose. He must be brought into the light before the stain of his granddam spreads."

Carys untied her apron to give her hands something to do other than wring the priest's neck like a chicken. Alys being born out of wedlock was a sin that had followed her and her mother Elin. For a time, Carys had been Elin's only visitor and brought the new mother supplies when others refused to help her through winter.

"The only stains here are the ones on my apron," she replied with an icy smile. "You aren't needed here, *offeiriad*. I'm sure Alys and Owain will call when the boy is ready for rites."

"Hold your tongue, woman. A *gwiddon* like you speaking so to a man of the cloth—your man will be ashamed of you. Your kind court demons, and I won't let you infect my flock."

A familiar outrage and old wound simmered in her chest. It gave her wicked pleasure to think that if he only knew what she truly was— if he saw that she resembled those demons he warned of, the old stories and memories of her kind warped—it'd make the man apoplectic. A little part of her wanted to drop the glamour, to let Arnall and all the others see.

It'd taken her some practice to accustom herself to Gavriel's magick and how to wield it. She couldn't do nearly the things he did with it, couldn't fold the realm around herself nor move enormous objects, but she could disguise herself. Upon reentering the human villages, she'd quickly had to master keeping up her human form with the glamour his magick could make her.

It would be so easy now, with her decades of practice, to let that mask slip. She could even make herself look more frightening than she was, really scare the priest and make his fearmongering a reality.

But she wouldn't.

She and Gavriel led a quiet, safe life at Caer Gwyn thanks to his magick and glamours. She wouldn't risk that for a moment's petty pleasure.

But oh, would it be a pleasure to see the shock and horror on the old coot's face.

Her wings twitched in irritation, but she held them still. The glamour could hide them from human eyes, but they were still there. Anyone could reach out and touch them, though they wouldn't see what it was they'd grasped. Gavriel's magick couldn't truly influence humans, just trick their eyes. He couldn't bend them to his will with magick, but then, he'd never need to, not with his—

"Is there a problem, *offeiriad?*"

The crowd that had watched the little spat with wide eyes, parted and dispersed in relief at the deep voice.

Gavriel let everyone move around him. Standing over a head taller than all the humans, his height and broad shoulders made him an imposing figure, looming above the crowd like an avenging angel Arnall was so fond of preaching about.

"Lord Gwynvael," Arnall grumped, sparing only the barest nod.

His predecessors had scraped and fawned over Gavriel as much as they despised and hissed at Carys, but she had to admit, Arnall was nothing if not consistent with his dislike. He was neither impressed nor intimidated by her mate.

Gavriel's magick had helped them maintain some presence in the villages as local landholders, though not liege lords. They saw to the nobles treating the common folk well where they could, but otherwise let the humans govern themselves. Still, it helped to have a modicum of respect when coming into the village. In the past centuries of conflict before Gruffydd ap Llywelyn unified the Cymry kingdoms, villagers had grown wary of outsiders. Not having to reestablish themselves in the communities again and again was a small blessing.

"Lady wife," said Gavriel, offering his arm.

"My lord husband," she replied, taking it.

Her lips twitched in a smile, but Gavriel's face remained severe. Lesser men had cowered under such a glare.

"You will speak to my wife with respect, Arnall."

"I must protect my flock, my lord. I cannot have her spreading pagan lies."

"She's a woman helping another woman in her time of need. She knows far more than you or me about what Alys needs at such a time."

"What she needs is—"

"Rest," finished Carys, "I completely agree. I shall check that they have what they need and then we can all leave them to get to know their son."

Arnall's face soured further, something Carys hadn't known was possible. Finally, looking like a turnip left too long in the sun, he huffed and went on his way back to the church.

She had to curl her tail around Gavriel's calf to keep it from lashing like an angry cat's.

"I sometimes think you like to provoke them."

"Maybe just a little . . ."

Gavriel snorted a quiet laugh. "Incorrigible. But if he ever . . ."

"He can't harm me. And if he tried, he'd find my claws."

Taking her hand and raising it to his lips, he kissed those claws. "I do enjoy how bloodthirsty you are when it comes to your charges."

She blushed, tucking a lock behind her ear. "Let me check in to see that Alys has everything she needs, then we'll go home."

"Yes. I've got news."

Interest piqued, Carys hurried to prepare Alys and the baby for the night, and warn her about Arnall's inevitable visit tomorrow. Looking happy about the reprieve, Alys settled down in her bed, cuddling her son close, as Carys went over a few simple instructions with Owain.

She left the couple in peace and took the hand Gavriel offered her.

They walked together through Harlech, returning greetings and well-wishes, and found the path northeast further into Eryri. Another trick of fae magick, only the two of them could find the path, and they strolled the mile back to Caer Gwyn hand in hand as Gavriel told her his news.

"I heard talk in Deganwy that the English king plans to rebuild the cathedral at Canterbury. Stonemasons from across the realm have been summoned, and the king is already collecting interesting statuary."

Carys looked up at him in surprise. Her mate hadn't involved himself in Cymry politics as he had in their first decades together, but he still travelled to the capitals. Although, since the destruction of Pengwern, he rarely strayed too far east into Powys. Instead, he frequented the Gwynedd capital of Deganwy, keeping apprised of any news. It was this way he'd been able to sniff out a few more of her kin.

Her heart beat a quick, excited rhythm.

A new lead, another chance . . .

But . . .

"Canterbury . . . that's all the way east across the island." Far farther than either of them had ever been, and Gavriel couldn't transport himself with magick somewhere he hadn't been before.

"Yes. It would be a long journey, and I don't know what might be found. But it's a chance. We could at least speak with the stonemasons, ask if anyone's seen statues that resemble your kin."

"We?"

Gavriel stopped, looking back at her. An afternoon breeze lifted his hair, making it glitter like starlight.

"I thought . . . you could come with me this time, *cariad*."

Carys swallowed, ready for the immediate denial to crawl up her throat, yet . . . it never came. The thought of leaving their home had terrified her for a long while—she'd never even been outside the everchanging borders of Wales, never stepped foot in the new united Saxon kingdom of England.

It all sounded so big and grand and terrifying.

And exciting.

She often scolded Arnall and his ilk for their narrow views, but could she truly say hers were all that much wider? Centuries now she'd lived while Albion changed around her. Whenever she stepped outside the borders of Caer Gwyn, it was into a whole new world.

Perhaps it was time to claim some of that world for herself.

Perhaps it was time to take some of this burden of freeing their people into her claws.

"All right," she said.

"Yes?" A smile spread across his face, making the greens and pinks of his opalescent skin gleam and popping that dimple in his cheek she so loved.

"Yes."

Catching her around the waist, Gavriel threw her over his shoulder and began bounding for their home.

"Gavriel! Put me down!"

"When we get to our bed, *cariad*. There's so much I want to do while we still have a bed beneath us."

III

A crisp breeze swirled across the canal, fluttering the ribbons knotted at the back of Carys's head. Her footsteps echoed off the stone and water, accompanied only by the hollow knock of a few docked gondolas.

Spring had taken a firm foothold here in the Floating City, but a chill still clung to the nights.

At least, it did in the quiet side streets. She found the cool air on her skin a delicious contrast to the hot press of bodies she'd escaped just a few moments before. At her back, Carnival was just getting started for the night and wine had been flowing for hours.

The slightly tangy scent of brackish water touched her nose as she navigated the narrow walkways along the canals. She counted doors to the colorful stone facades of Venezia's rich and important *palazzi*, keeping track of how far she'd come and how far she had to go.

Excitement thrummed in her veins as she slipped between shadows, the tall Venetian windows barely catching her dark reflection as she hurried past. Her heavy brocade skirts swished against her legs, a sensation she still found delightful after growing so used to the simple dresses or braies she wore at home.

Finding the door she needed, Carys tipped back the wide brim of her velvet mantle to see how high she may need to climb. The *palazzi* sat like preening birds on a branch, all vibrant and colorful and cramped together. The space between this *palazzo* and the next was narrower than she was tall, meaning she could climb it. Unless . . .

Slinking around back, Carys found what she was after. An unlocked door.

She slipped inside and locked the door behind her so no servant would be scolded when the master found out.

The interior, like the streets outside, was abandoned. Everyone flocked to Carnival, masters and servants alike, not wanting to miss the revelry and debauchery. In fact, she rather missed it herself.

Her pulse pounded at her neck, that excitement only growing as she found a staircase up further into the house. She tip-toed past a door with candlelight glowing underneath and blushed as she passed another with moans and grunting behind it.

The sounds set her heart to racing even faster, that thrumming pulsing now not just in her neck but her breasts and core, too.

They'd made a game of it this time. Gavriel had learned of at least two interesting new sculptures setting the cultured elite abuzz. Brought in specifically for the revel of Carnival, two rival merchants were eager to show off their new pieces. Streets apart, they'd decided to confirm the statues were her kin one night and secret them away the next. Only, it didn't take both of them to sneak inside a human home.

Carys crept through the house to the ornate parlor on the third floor. Stuffed with art and heavy velvets, the room nearly absorbed the meager light eking in from the canal outside. The plush carpets silenced her footfalls as she inspected the collection of statuary gathered at the east wall.

Her breath caught at the sight of arching horns and claw-tipped wings. There she was. A female guardian snarled at her with stone fangs, visible even beneath the gossamer veil thrown over her head. Carys drew it back with a claw, looking into the empty eyes of her kin.

"Hello, sister," she whispered. The female wasn't her blood-kin, and her face wasn't familiar in the dark of the shadows and millennium since the curse was cast, but she was her sister nevertheless. "I've come to take you home. Just one more night, and then you return to our kin."

She kissed the female's cheek then replaced the veil.

One at least. It made the journey here and years spent in the south all the more worth it.

She'd enjoyed their time in the Italian states, delighted in their little villa outside Firenze that now burst with art and beauty. She had pieces from many of the premier Italian painters and sculptors—though she still remembered haggling with Michelangelo with a horrified shudder.

But she missed her home. Caer Gwyn always welcomed them home with a warmth she found nowhere else. Her first venture past the Welsh borders had been a success, and she and Gavriel had returned with two of her kin in time to watch in horror as the island was invaded yet again by the Norman kings. She and Gavriel had done what they could in the intervening centuries, had supported Gruffudd ap Cynan, Llywelyn the Great, and Owain Glyndwr against the Norman and English advances.

After centuries of war and strife, the kingships of the Cymry died with Glyndwr.

Now, the English kings called their sons Prince of Wales.

Carys's heart bled for her land, but there was nothing she and Gavriel could do. When the last of the dead had been laid to rest, they both knew it was time to go somewhere new, somewhere far away.

They'd travelled to Paris, Amsterdam, and Vienna. They'd gone to the east, following the footsteps of pilgrims to Israel and then onwards to Egypt. They'd wandered the markets of Constantinople and sailed through the islands of the Aegean. Something about the warm valleys of Italia had finally called to them, and they'd settled for a time here.

Perhaps, now that she thought about it, she liked it so much because it reminded her of home. So many small kingdoms and self-important princes vying for lands they could never hope to hold. The language was sometimes the only thing uniting the many lands of Italia, and it made her think of all the lordlings and skirmishes for bits of land around Caer Gwyn.

Hiraeth.

That's what the Cymry called it.

She longed for home.

Now, with the discovery of her kin, it would be a true homecoming.

"We'll be home soon, the both of us," she promised.

But first, she had to find her mate . . . or let him find her.

With a devilish grin, Carys opened a window and glided down to the street below.

The game was on.

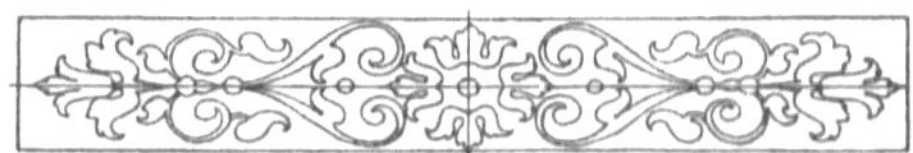

The spectacle of Carnival erupted in the main streets and *piazze* of Venezia, a feast for all her senses. Vendors plied roasted meats and cheeses on sticks, and sweet wines flowed like water through the canals. Torches and bonfires banished the thick darkness of night, and the fire-eaters spat flame to resounding applause. Musicians plucked at their lutes and lyres, filling the air with raucous melodies that battled and blended. Feathers and velvets brushed past her as the Venetians moved down the busy streets, frolicking in the celebration.

Carys let herself be taken with the tide of revelers, pulling back her mantle hood so as not to miss a thing.

Everywhere, white masks concealed faces behind exaggerated noses and brows. Wide, excited eyes darted in the eye holes, the fire-eaters' flames catching in the whites. Husbands and wives parted in the crowd, and secret lovers found each other. Lords donned their butlers' coats and footmen swaggered in their masters' tricorne hats. A jester rode a nag backwards, and more than one child rode a bleating goat through the crowd.

Revelers gathered in groups to laugh and joke, and down a side street she spied a skit being put on to loud approval from its audience. Others slipped in and out of the crowd, looking for a private little corner—though not all waited to find privacy in the shadows. Couples of all kinds, young and old, man and woman, men, women, three, four, all sought pleasure with wandering mouths and writhing hips, not caring who saw.

She caught the eye of a woman pinned against the near façade, arm clutching at the stone face as her lover hitched her leg higher up his hip. His bare buttocks flexed as he hammered inside her, and the woman smiled cheekily at Carys before throwing her head back and crying out in ecstasy.

The barest hint of a familiar scent drew Carys out of her aroused blush, and she looked about the crowd.

There, back at the last bridge, stood a figure much taller than the rest.

Grinning, Carys ducked back into the crowd.

She didn't hasten her steps, didn't give any sign that she knew the chase was afoot.

The feeling of hungry eyes watching her every movement had her heart thundering in her chest and nipples tightening against the neckline of her gown.

A hand reached out and caught her wrist, pulling her out of the flow of the crowd.

The wrong hand.

A strange man smiled down at her, eyes slightly bleary from too much wine.

"Dance with me," he said, smiling in a way that may have charmed human women.

"You'd best let me be, *signor*." She pulled his hand away and patted his chest. "I'm not alone tonight."

He blinked at her in bafflement, and she spun away just as a looming figure descended on the drunkard. The man whimpered and Carys made her escape.

She didn't feel the eyes again until the next street. Looking back across the bridge, she saw the tall, mysterious figure on the other side, eyes shadowed behind a white mask. The intensity of his gaze had her wings fluttering, and she blew him a kiss across the canal.

Carys weaved between revelers, their laughs and masks blending into a symphony of celebration that set her blood alight. She picked up her skirts and twirled to the music with other dancing women, she took the goblet of wine handed to her, she unpinned some of the heavy curls from her head.

And she kept just ahead of him.

She felt him, oh she always felt him, his carnal intensity following her wherever she went. She danced just for him, drank to his name, and let free her curls to gleam in the firelight just for him.

He remained in the shadows, on the periphery, always just out of sight, but she knew he was there. When he darted closer, she danced away, breathless with delight at his delicious growls.

He pursued her through the parade and revelry, through the canals and *piazze*. She let him chase her around the Campanile and through the Piazza San Marco. Past basilicas and *palazzi*, past statues and fountains and gardens she danced, him never more than a few paces behind.

It was on a dark, quiet street that she let him finally catch her.

She awaited him at the crest of the canal bridge, breaths coming fast as he melted from the crowd, a shadow topped with a tricorne hat. A mask covered his face from lips to brow, but moonlight caught in the quicksilver of his eyes.

He mounted the bridge slowly, approaching as though she'd run from him again.

Instead, she leaned against the railing, setting her hands on the cool stone.

"It isn't safe to leave the celebration, *signora*," he said, his rumbling voice echoing behind his mask.

"Why not?" she asked, chest tight with anticipation as he drew ever closer, a predator stalking its prey.

"Dangerous things lurk in the shadows."

"Like demons?"

"Worse."

"Husbands?"

She caught part of his wicked smile and gasped when he caught her by the hip to draw her to him. Even through her heavy skirts she felt his heat and hardness. Their masks clacked together when his mouth swooped to claim hers in a hungry kiss, and she felt just how desperate their little game had rendered him.

His hands were rough and quick, hitching her skirts up to her hips.

"You're fortunate it's Carnival, thinking to take such liberties, *signor*," she sighed as he pressed hot, open-mouthed kisses to her neck and chest.

"I'll be taking much more than liberties, *signora*," he promised in that wicked, lyrical purr she so loved.

Ripping his mask away, Gavriel flashed her a smile full of fang before he descended on her breasts. He teased a nipple free of her bodice, lashing it with his tongue. Writhing in his arms, she welcomed the thigh he thrust between her legs. Grinding down, she finally found the friction she'd been craving.

"Gavriel," she moaned.

"Yes, *cariad*," he murmured.

Skirts about her waist, he set her on the bridge railing and drew her legs around him. Fluttering kisses traced where her mask met her cheek as his hands worked the front of his breeches free. Sharing gasps and moans, he plunged inside her.

Locking her ankles at the small of his back and setting her claws in the softness of his cloak, Carys's head fell back, golden curls tumbling towards the gentle water of the canal. Kisses rained down the column of her throat, and high above them, the boom of fireworks awoke the night.

Carys opened her eyes to a bright waterfall of colors and smiled. For one glorious moment, the night was as bright as the day, lit up in warmth and color and hope.

She clutched her mate tight, making him groan, and set her little fangs at his throat.

He grunted with release, and she tumbled down with him, lit like fireworks.

IV

1763
Hillcrest, Shropshire, England

The ring of metal meeting metal filled the morning, and the meadow held its breath to see how their little duel would play out.

Gavriel parried his mate's next attack, sending her and her vicious little rapier dancing backward. She twirled, wings flapping to keep him away, until she could get her posture again. She brandished her sword at him with a gleefully evil smile that would've worried him were he not nearly immortal.

He smiled at her, showing off his fangs in that way he knew drove her mad—in every sense.

Her little nostrils flared and then she was at him again with hard, swinging blows that had him dancing back himself. That feral part of him that lived for his mate was so damn proud. His *cariad* was strong, resilient, and lethal, and it set his blood to boiling to watch her twirl and strike and imagine her inflicting such damage on any would-be assailant. A human wouldn't know what they'd incurred before it was too late, and the thought had him sweating under the bright morning sun.

The spring day was unseasonably warm, but their spar was too delicious to retreat back to the house just yet. One of the many things he liked about this new English home of theirs was the flat sparring field he'd laid just for mornings like this.

It'd taken him decades to finally convince Carys to reside in England. For all that they didn't interfere with human affairs much, only lending aid to those who needed it when they could, her dislike of the English was ancient and unyielding. Still, it had pleased both of them to claim the lands that had once been Pengwern. In what the English now considered Shropshire, on lands that had once belonged to the Cymry and Pengwern, they built a fine manor house in the newest style and filled it with their many treasures, including Carys's kin.

That had taken even more convincing, but finally, after so many centuries of no luck, they'd been left with nothing else to try. Set up as another palatial country estate, their home of Hillcrest lured the rich and the fashionable of British and European society to admire their collection of worldly treasure and unique statuary. Already they'd garnered new leads on other statues like theirs in collections in Bavaria, Istanbul, and Kyiv.

And as each new human strolled past, Gavriel kept a small hope that maybe, maybe it would finally be time . . .

They now held over a hundred of Carys's kin. Kept together for decades in the safety of Caer Gwyn, none had awoken. None were mates. As the mate bond was what had ultimately freed Gavriel of his tether to the Underhill, he'd suspected for a long while now that that bond could perhaps be the answer to Titania's curse—but nothing happened with the guardians put together. Either he was wrong . . . or the guardians' mates weren't guardians at all.

Then again, he could be wrong.

They'd yet to formulate a new strategy to try, so they were left to play host to this Lord and that Viscount and all manner of society ladies. And while they waited for the next visit, Gavriel enjoyed letting his little mate trounce him.

"You must always remember that your size will be a disadvantage," he said in his best didactic tone. Her annoyed grumble made him grin; he'd said such to her many times, in many languages, over many spars. "Take your advantages where you can."

Their swords met in a sharp clap, and Gavriel couldn't help watching the bead of sweat sliding down between her breasts. The white cotton clung to her dewy skin, nearly obscene in how it contoured to her figure.

Another wicked smile was his only warning, and then her claws were pulling her collar down, revealing one luscious breast. Flushed even pinker with their exertion, her skin was luminous in the daylight. She cupped her breast, claws just sinking into the pillowy flesh, and that pert pink nipple made his mouth run dry.

"Ha!" With a whirl, she knocked the sword from his hand.

Lust dulled his reactions, and he almost growled when she levelled the sharp tip of her rapier at his throat and tucked herself away from his sight.

"Evil vixen," he accused.

She preened.

"Do you yield, sir?"

"Never." Not when he remembered their little wager before beginning—winner decided their afternoon activities—and now he was more determined than ever to win it.

He knocked away her sword with the back of his wrist and dove for his weapon. She was on him in a moment, and they danced across the practice field as the sun drew higher in the sky.

Now and then he caught a capped head peeking out windows at them. With a house the size of Hillcrest and a millennium of treasures in their care, they did need to keep a small human staff. He paid them all handsomely, knowing all the eccentricities they'd witness from their odd Welsh lord and lady. Dueling all morning wasn't out of the ordinary; nor was the lady of the house walking about in just a shirt and breeches, a whole kennel of devoted dogs behind her; nor that many in the lord's collection of fine swords he'd made himself in the forge he'd added to the back of the house.

When Mrs. Sully, their current housekeeper, finally marched outside and waved a kerchief at him, Gavriel decided it was time to claim his boon. If they didn't come in and eat their luncheon, Mrs. Sully would have a fit, and that meant no dessert after dinner. Not a consequence Gavriel could live with.

In a few decisive moves, he drove Carys to the edge of the field. She knew his game; they'd had so many centuries to learn every trick, every feint.

He thought of her flashing him her breast and smiled hungrily.

Oh, she still surprised him, all these centuries later.

With a flourish, he sent her rapier spinning out of her hand and her back spinning into his front. The flat of his sword held perpendicular to her middle, he traced the pointed tip of her pink ear with his nose and hummed smugly.

"Do you yield, madame?"

She huffed. "Just for today."

"And you agree I win?"

Carys peered up at him, long lashes nearly touching her brows. He couldn't help caressing the long column of her throat with gentle fingertips. Her eyes darkened with lust and her breathing drew deeper, breasts rising as if they wanted to be free. He wanted that, too.

"Yes."

"Then you know what I want."

"What about the Ashmoores?"

"They don't arrive until six o'clock."

She hummed, considering, and he let his fingertips stray lower.

"Very well," she said breathily, making him press his hips to her backside. "I'm an honorable female, I keep my word."

"Wear the green gown," he rumbled, nipping at her ear. "And be quick. Or else we'll give Mrs. Sully an eyeful."

"Oh dear. Poor Mrs. Sully has already seen quite enough for one human lifetime."

Heart fluttering faster than birdwings, Carys picked up her skirts and dashed through the forest. Her talons dug into the rich earth, kicking up pebbles and leaves.

She wouldn't make it too hard for him. Not that he ever needed her help—he preferred it when she drew out the chase. But she was feeling a little too needy today.

Perhaps it was the unseasonable warmth and the buzz of all the growing things coming alive again in spring. Perhaps it was their sparring with swords and tongues.

It was most certainly that they played their most favorite game now.

Duties and obligations and plans forgotten, she lost herself to the woods, bounding over streams and roots and boulders. Doves and quails flapped hurriedly to get out of her way, rabbits hopping for their dens and squirrels chittering from their branches.

Her skirts and stays didn't hamper her much as she wended through the trees, the tension of the neckline and soft rasp of the cloth adding another level of sensation.

The back of her neck prickled, and the magick inside her shivered in delight.

He's close.

Lengthening her stride, Carys changed directions, hurrying past familiar outcroppings and newly downed trees. Flower petals brushed her skirts, their scents bursting through the air to obscure her trail.

At least, to the mortal hunter.

The eyes of the forest watched her, and she could feel him gaining speed, could feel the heat of his hunger at her back.

She caught a flash of opalescent gleam in the corner of her eye and changed course.

When he did it again, she realized where she was being herded.

She'd just crossed into the little meadow tucked deep in the woods when arms clasped around her from behind. With a gasp, she went tumbling to the ground, crushing grass and larkspurs beneath her.

She rolled to her back and gazed up at the figure looming over her.

The most handsome male she'd ever seen watched her with dark, hungry eyes. Naked gray skin shone with pinks and greens in the sunlight filtering in to the forest floor, the light catching on the wicked points of his long ears and the silver hoops studding the shell. Wild hair hung in a silver curtain from his head, a match to the wildness in those quicksilver eyes that glittered like a pond in sunlight.

Beautiful and terrible, he was every story the humans told of forest spirits and silver-tongued fairies come to life.

He caged her in with his body, the corded muscles of his arms taut as he held himself above her and devoured her with his glittering gaze.

"Who are you to trespass in my woods?" he asked, voice as deep as the roots of the forest.

"Unhand me," she gasped. "How dare you accost the Lady of Hillcrest?"

"Straying into my woods comes at a price, *mo tè bhòidheach*."

She shivered again hearing the rough brogue. "I cannot trespass on my own lands. My husband is the Lord of Hillcrest."

"What is your husband's claim to mine? I am more ancient than your fine house on the hill, older than the trees around us. They are all mine, as is everything that passes here."

Slowly, so slowly, he lowered his head to her, drawing in a deep breath from her neck, just where her pulse beat wildly at her throat.

"I watched you run through my woods," he whispered to her, lips barely grazing her skin. "You were so free, so wild. You yearn for freedom outside that house on the hill and all your finery."

Deft fingers began unlacing the ribbons of her stays, loosening her bodice just enough that with a sharp tug, her breasts spilled free of her gown. He laved the tops of her breasts with his hot tongue, drawing moans and gasps as she rocked beneath him. Head thrown back, she dug her fingers in that wild hair and felt the inhuman shape of his ears.

He kissed her throat, her chin, her cheeks.

"Can you pay the price, female? For trespassing in my woods?"

He freed the last knot of her stays and ran his hand down her leg to gather great handfuls of her voluminous skirts. Bunched at her hip, she moaned at the heat of his palm as it clasped her stockinged thigh and toyed with the bows of her garters.

"Or perhaps you wanted to be caught? Perhaps you entered my domain knowing what I would demand, wanting what I would give . . ."

"My husband . . ."

He quelled her with a kiss that was all tongue and teeth, sharp nips and swirling laves, as if he would devour her.

"There is only you and I, female. Nothing else. But perhaps this will decide you."

Quicker than she could see, her skirts went flying up to her middle and he pulled her legs as far apart as they could go. Tangling his fingers in one of her garters, his mouth closed around her center. His tongue speared through her wet folds, finding her sensitive nub with predatory intent. It was brutal, his hands firm as he kept her there under his mouth and all the pleasure he thrust upon her.

Her back bowed and she couldn't help her wail of ecstasy. She went flying when his lips closed around her nub and sucked.

Starbursts blinded her, and she clutched at the grasses and flowers beneath her for something to hold onto.

Her body throbbed like an exposed nerve, not yet satiated even though she'd just peaked. His looming figure blighted out the sunlight above her, those hungry eyes trained on her as she panted, breasts rising and falling with her rapid breaths.

"Make your choice, female," he murmured, his voice thrumming through her like thunder across a valley.

"Yes," she whispered, "yes."

He fell upon her like a tempest, all open-mouthed kisses and strong, seeking fingers. He took her mouth in a searing kiss, making her taste herself and take his tongue and savage passion. She scraped her nails through his hair as he kissed down her neck and chest to claim a breast. He tugged at her nipple, bordering on pain, and she whimpered in delight.

His dark chuckle filled her up as surely as his fingers as he slid two inside her. The wet sounds he drew from her might have made her blush if she'd had the time or sense to be ashamed, but there wasn't time, not when the flat of his thumb stroked broad circles over her nub.

She told him with grasping hands and rocking hips that she was close, so close.

The hot head of his cock slid against her aching flesh, and her mouth fell open at the shock of his heat. He teased her with short, brutal thrusts and taps to her nub as he glided through her slick.

"Please," she begged, "please please please . . ."

A darkly pleased, wholly male sound reverberated in his chest, and then he was thrusting inside, claiming every inch of her.

It was all she needed to fly again. Her pleasure came sharp, nearly painful, as she clutched at his cock, milking it as he held still inside her. She writhed beneath his hands that fondled and squeezed and thumbed her breasts and nub. His touch was everywhere, as if he had more than two hands. She felt it along her neck, at her pulse, nipping at her earlobe. Warm cascades rolled against her lips and nipples, and even though he didn't move a muscle, that strong, dangerous body held taut above her, something teased at her nub in whispering little strokes.

Magick.

With a wicked smile, he didn't wait for her to descend from the heights of her pleasure. Palms splayed over her hips and skirts, he sat back on his ankles and drew her up his body. Her stockings rasped against his skin, and her backside met the unyielding muscle of his thighs.

"Everything in the forest is mine," he growled. "You are *mine*."

"Yes," she cried.

"Again."

"Yes! Yours!"

Fingers digging into her hips, he slammed their hips together with a wet smack, and it was all she could do to hold onto a shred of her sanity. His hips rolled and lashed like waves in a storm, crashing and never-ending. His cock speared her with every thrust, hollowing her out until she was nothing but the next drag of his cockhead, next wave of lust.

"Show me your pretty breasts," he rumbled, eyes fixed on her even as their bodies crashed together.

She filled her hands with her soft flesh, kneading them and pushing them up to show off the strained, puckered nipples. He grunted in approval, his pace somehow gaining speed. Her backside bounced off his thighs in wet slaps, her slick soaking his cock.

Her skin sparked and tingled and everywhere throbbed for more. She'd barely recovered from her last peak when he was driving her higher, past the point of pleasure into something more searing, more mind-numbingly delicious. She pulsed and clutched around him, a body that could only feel.

"Come for me, *mo tè bhòidheach*. Show me just how wild you can be."

She did—screaming to the sky, she came apart at the seams. He joined her, his roar a harmony to hers as the forest watched their passion crest. It seemed to go on forever, a tidal wave of pleasure that pooled inside her and drenched every part of her, finding every nook and niche and hidden part.

But eventually, the forest sounds came back to her, nearly drowned out by their heavy panting.

Gavriel slid forward, catching himself on a hand. His long hair fell around them, a wave of warm amber and sandalwood and moss saturating her senses. They stared at one another for a long while, their breaths mixing and harmonizing.

When she smiled and opened her arms to him, he eased down to her with a satisfied sigh. His softening cock still throbbed inside her, but his kisses and caresses were gentle. His lips found hers, and they kissed softly in the meadow for another long while, content to be and stay exactly as they were.

"I didn't hurt you?" he asked after a time.

"Never."

He hummed in relief and buried his head in her neck.

"That should teach you to tempt the god of the forest."

Carys threw back her head and laughed.

1816
Mayfair, London, England

Smoke plumes rose lazily from cigars dangling from idle lips, adding a hazy hint of spice to the air. The light in the sumptuous cardroom had drawn low with the advent of night, the sconces all lit and candelabras placed about the room. The long shadows didn't hide the mortified curiosity of the onlookers to his little game, nor the dangerous scowl Lord Elgin levelled at Gavriel from across the card table.

This night and this damnable whist game had gone on for far too long, and Gavriel's patience was nearing its end. Lord Elgin had wished to play and Gavriel wished to buy a statue from him. So they'd sat down to a game, which had become two, which had become more as Gavriel let the Scottish lord win a few hands.

Elgin's eyes had gleamed avariciously as he pocketed the notes, but the winnings only whetted his appetite. Rather than agreeing to sell Gavriel the statue he wanted, Elgin insisted on more port, more cards, more rounds.

They'd been here two hours at least, and he suspected he may be even further from securing another of his *cariad's* kin.

The thought of his lovely mate irritated his impatience. He'd left her to the mercies of the ballroom and their hostess, Lady Nelson. Over the last century, he and Carys had made a name for themselves as a family of collectors, and that meant visiting London, the center spoke of the empire. The ton hadn't held back its curiosity over the new Lord and Lady Gwynvael and their fantastical collection of treasures. The invitations had flowed, and this was their sixth year of entertaining a London season, on the hunt for Carys's kin and any works that chronicled the early history of Albion. So far, they'd been disappointed.

And then, finally, a spot of good news. Lord and Lady Elgin's divorce was the talk of London—while the earl had been away stealing marbles and other treasures in Greece, his own friend had stolen his wife's heart back home. The separation was, according to all the best gossip, staggeringly expensive.

Gavriel didn't doubt it, what with the harsh lines carved into Elgin's tanned face. In a matter of three years, the man had gone from aspirations of opening a private museum of acquired Greek marbles to sitting in smoky cardrooms hoarding pound notes.

But Elgin's loss would be Gavriel's gain.

At least, that had been the plan two hours ago.

He'd tried the soft way, tried endearing himself to Elgin. Let the man win a few rounds, down a few glasses of port, and then settle in to haggle price on the statue Gavriel had glimpsed on an earlier tour of the collection with Carys. Word was that his competition was the British government itself, but Elgin had stubbornly refused the crown's first offer.

If Elgin wouldn't take Gavriel's more than generous offer, either, then he'd have to do this the harder, and much more fun way.

Gavriel started winning. Not by much at first, oh no, and even allowed Elgin to win a round to calm the man's nerves.

But the cards and the port kept coming, and so did Gavriel. Their partners fled before the sums could grow any higher. They changed to piquet at Elgin's insistence, a game Gavriel much preferred. He and Carys had wiled away many rainy English afternoons playing piquet, and Elgin's was nothing to his mate's skill. Of course, Elgin didn't figure this out until several hands in.

Loosening the knot of the cream cravat at his neck, Gavriel arranged his fresh hand of cards and waved for Elgin to begin.

The lord hesitated.

As well he should, already six-hundred pounds indebted.

Gavriel watched patiently as the wheels and cogs of the lord's mind worked through the haze of the port. In his inaction, most of the other men in the cardroom gave up the pretense of billiards or conversation and drew closer to the match.

Elgin's shoulders tensed feeling all the curious eyes on their game. He took a long breath, eyes flicking to the faces gathering round.

A slow smile spread across his face, something Gavriel didn't like.

Finally, Elgin picked up his hand and surveyed his cards.

Setting them down again, Elgin folded his fingers on the table and smiled beatifically at Gavriel.

"My lord, we are all sporting gentlemen here. What say you to a more interesting bet?"

Gavriel arched a brow. Ah, here it came. Elgin had finally had enough and would try to bet his way out of their gamble.

"I'm intrigued, sir," Gavriel said.

"This round shan't be for notes but for things much more precious. If you win, you may select any of my statues you wish." The men around them murmured, and even Gavriel leaned in a little further, truly intrigued. An all or nothing bet made a twisted sort of sense when Elgin stood to lose another hundred pounds to their game.

"And should I lose?"

Elgin's lips twitched in an ugly grin. "Then I shall take Lady Gwynvael on another tour of my collection. A private tour."

His ears rang with how devastatingly fast his patience snapped.

The stupid human did not see. Or perhaps did not care.

"They say you are so often locked away studying your treasures, sir. Always lost in a book. I'm sure your wife would welcome a day of enjoyment. The marbles are indeed . . . stimulating."

That bestial, howling part of him roared, demanding retribution, *violence*, at such an insult. He held his body tense and unmoving, working to conceal the viciousness from his face—but couldn't keep it from gleaming in his eyes.

The crowd around them hushed, and even in the soft light of the red-velveted cardroom and under his tanned skin, Elgin paled.

"Your wife is a bonny woman, if you had not noticed, my lord. She deserves to be taken out and enjoyed."

The man didn't truly want the bet, only made it so outrageous that Gavriel would refuse. He knew this—and it was the only thought that kept him from lunging across the table to strangle Elgin.

The men waited with bated breath for Gavriel's refusal, for Gavriel's outrage.

He let them all hang on it, deriving wicked pleasure from their unease. Morbid curiosity kept them near, though many looked as though they wished to leave. Whatever happened, it wouldn't be good.

No, it would not.

"Very well," Gavriel said slowly. "A statue for a day with my wife."

The room let out a gasp, and Elgin's mouth fell open. An agreement, now binding on their word as gentlemen, in a room full of them.

"I believe it's your hand, sir," said Gavriel tightly.

Hands trembling, Elgin picked up his cards. He blinked, likely unseeing, and did nothing for a long moment.

Once he made his first move, Gavriel had no mercy.

They moved through the sets of the game at a steady pace, as if Elgin knew there was now no escape. They each discarded cards and declared their hands. Points were tallied, and with every one Gavriel scored, another line creased Elgin's face.

It didn't take long, a mercy kill of sorts.

Gavriel showed his final hand and took the game.

The room shuddered, relieved and horrified. More than one man retreated as quickly as he could for the safety of the ballroom.

Elgin stared at the card table as Gavriel rose and straightened his waistcoat. The man's defeat was too delicious not to enjoy, but he gave himself only a moment. Planting a hand on the table and the massacre of their cards, Gavriel loomed over Elgin.

"Speak my wife's name again and I'll cut the tongue from your mouth. Look at her again and I'll pluck the eyes from your head. Do you understand me?"

Elgin's throat bobbed as he swallowed, and with lips pursed in sour defeat, he nodded.

"Excellent. Lady Gwynvael and I shall be round at nine o'clock tomorrow to select the statue she wants." He couldn't give Elgin time to revisit the government's offer, as he no doubt would have to.

Perhaps he could have forgiven the six-hundred pounds in his winnings; he'd pay double for one of his mate's kin. But his own viciousness wouldn't allow it, and he took great pleasure in leaving the cardroom and Lord Elgin to his loss.

It was time he found his *cariad*.

She was, of course, a vision of loveliness. Gavriel prowled the ballroom until he spotted her, wandering the fringes of the crowd. She kept to the groups of married women, all left to idle as their husbands gambled and their children danced and flirted. Near them, but not quite a part.

Carys stood out like the first blooms of spring amidst the last winter frosts. Against a background of staid greens and blues and whites, her dusky pink gown gave her all the colors of a sunset, blushes and golds and a hint of lilac. To the human eye, she cut a somewhat tall, buxom figure, big curls of blonde hair piled atop her head. The pink of her gown and diamonds glittering at her throat, dangling from her ears, and twinkling in the luscious waves of her hair lent her a glow that all the other women lacked. Pale under their powders, they looked ghostly compared to the soft warmth of his mate's human skin, tanned from their days in the sun.

He'd more than once overheard comments whispered under cupped hands how odd it was—had the Lady Gwynvael truly never heard of parasols or sleeves?

Just jealousy speaking, he was sure of it.

He couldn't blame them, not when she outshone everyone and everything in the room, even in her human disguise.

Gavriel saw her true colors, and it gave him no end of delight to see her deftly weave through the crowd, wings bending to avoid being touched, her curls and diamonds wound expertly around her precious little horns. The soft, warm hues of peaches and sunsets and flowers, she was all the best things.

He didn't miss the two small lines between her brows, though. The night had been arduous and he'd been apart from her too long. As he began making his way for her across the ballroom, he watched her eyes flick to a group of whispering women. She nodded to them and continued on her way, but when she thought they wouldn't see, drew her diaphanous shawl higher on her shoulders to hide away some of her peachy flesh.

A tragedy.

His mate hadn't been quiet about her dislike of this era's fashions. She'd grown fond of fuller skirts and the supportive shape of stays. More than once, he'd sat patiently as she ranted about the unflattering empire silhouette—how the straight skirts were either too tight on her generous hips and thighs or made her a "shapeless column" when more fabric was added. The high waist either cut across her breasts (another tragedy) or left them on display when it sat at her ribs.

Gavriel didn't mind listening in the slightest, not when she argued her case by grabbing and manipulating her breasts to show him this problem or that. It always ended the same way—she made her modifications and he kissed his way across all the delectable exposed skin.

She didn't see what he did, how eyes followed her wherever she went. The somewhat shapeless silhouette couldn't truly hide her, the curve of her hips evident with every swaying step. She played with the diamond pendant at her chest absently, drawing every male eye to the perfection of her breasts.

A growl worked up his throat.

Between all the stares and Elgin's wager, he wanted to hurry his mate somewhere safe and private and under him.

But he knew her bored misery when he saw it. There was one last thing they had to do.

He met her on the east side of the ballroom just as the quartet finished a jaunty quadrillion. A round of applause went up as couples quitted the floor and the musicians arranged their sheet music.

She smiled in relief to see him, not surprised when he appeared before her.

"Thank the goddesses," she muttered, happily burrowing under his arm. She laid her cheek against his chest and hummed. "I was beginning to believe you'd retired home without me."

"Never."

She grinned. "I know." Lifting her chin so she could see his face, she blinked those golden eyes at him. "How did you fare?"

He couldn't help his slow smile, one that was only for her. There was nothing in this realm or any other like telling his mate he'd found another of her kind. Slipping his arm around her, he dipped his head and captured her lips in a kiss that, chaste as it was for them, still caused murmurs around them.

Six years and the ton was still shocked with how besotted the Lord and Lady Gwynvael were with each other.

"We collect it tomorrow."

Carys cupped his face in her little hand, smoothing her thumb over his cheek. "Thank you, *fy annwyl*," she whispered to him.

"Anything, my darling," he whispered back. "Anything." He took her hand and brought it to his lips, kissing every fingertip, before securing it at his elbow. "But I would ask a boon."

"Oh?" She arched a brow at him, some of her tiredness ebbing away.

"Dance with me?"

She looked about, watching the other couples gather as the first notes of a waltz began to fill the room. Humans twirled past, all flowing skirts and rigid arms.

He pressed his hand more firmly into the small of her back.

Carys grinned. "I think you like setting tongues to wagging."

"What I like is holding my mate close."

A blush deepened the pink of her cheeks, and with a nod, she let him lead her out onto the ballroom floor.

Gavriel took her hand in one of his and filled his other with the softness of her waist. He led her through the first steps, and with every spin, they drew closer and closer. It wasn't long before they danced just how he wanted, with his hand at the small of her back, scandalously close to her lush backside, and her breasts crushed to his chest.

He twirled them with the human couples, not caring that people stared and whispered. The mercurial opinion of the ton didn't matter, only his mate and her happy, effervescent smile did.

Her hand slid from his shoulder down to rest on his chest, just over the heart that beat solely for her.

There had been times in the intervening centuries that nearly broke him. He'd lost friends, he'd lost faith. They'd caught not even a hint of where Morrígan may lie, and though their collection of guardians slowly grew, they were all still encased in their stone prisons. At times it felt as though the task Rhiannon had set him was folly. That he was destined to fail his people and his mate's, too.

But then Carys smiled at him, stirring his magick and setting his soul alight, and he was reminded that hope wasn't lost—not so long as he stayed standing beside this beautiful creature.

Something had brought them together, all those centuries ago. He had to trust that that same something would reveal how to help their peoples, too.

VI

The light from thousands of candles illuminated *le nouvel Opéra de Paris*, making it glow brighter than the dawn. Cast in golden hues, the marble of the grand staircase gleamed, the delicate veins catching the light in subtle twinkles. Gold leaf glittered between richly painted scenes and exquisitely tooled mosaics, and statues so lifelike they almost blended with the crowd stood sentinel throughout the palatial space.

Carys hummed under her breath at the sheer opulence of the new Paris Opera, or the Palais Garnier as many had taken to calling it, after the architect who envisioned such splendid sumptuousness. She and Gavriel had come with the mission to find out if any of the statuary used to decorate both the ornate exterior and lavish interior were in fact her kin—they'd plucked more than one guardian off of Parisian cathedrals and palaces before—but she was more than happy to take in the opera while they did.

When she'd heard they were putting on Puccini's newest opera, she insisted they visit.

For all its stone and metal, the grand entrance and staircase glowed with warmth, in no small part from the jovial buzz of the crowd slowly meandering up the steps, splitting up either side of the staircase to the Grand Foyer. Jewelry glittered and silks gleamed in the soft light, adding a dizzying, dazzling air to the night.

Handing his hat and their gloves to an attendant, Gavriel gave her a small grin and led them deeper into the opera house. The cool slap of shoes on marble made her think of their years spent in Italy.

Carys ran a hand down her dress, the crimson silk flowing over her like wine. She'd always taken a liking to fashions and dressing the part of a fine human lady, though some eras had vexed her more than others. Nothing compared to a simple shirt and comfortable pair of trousers to tuck them in to, but when she and Gavriel did venture out into society, even after a thousand years, she got a little thrill putting on a pretty dress.

The puff of her gathered sleeves flattered the curves of her arms, and she'd enjoyed adding the black lace sleeves that frilled at her wrists beneath bracelets of rubies and diamonds. A lace collar at her throat and silk rose in her hair had been fanciful little touches she decided upon a few moments before they left.

They hadn't strolled the busy streets of bourgeois Paris in a long while, and though they often preferred the quiet of their homes scattered across Europe, every now and then, it was a delight to immerse themselves in the bustle of mortal life. It could be difficult to engage with the human world, and she and Gavriel both had learned over centuries the heartache of losing friends and companions. They chose their human friends and associates carefully.

But the tides of time had brought them to Paris to finally see the exquisite New Opera, and tonight, even if they didn't find one of her kin, Carys was determined to enjoy herself.

She hugged the arm she held, peeking up at her handsome mate. He was devastating in his dark coat trimmed in golden threads, crimson ascot pinned with a Welsh dragon pendant shaped from a single ruby, and brocade waistcoat emphasizing his lithe form. Human eyes would see a stylish gentleman with hair parted and swept back from his sharp face, but Carys enjoyed the silvery fall of his true hair, the top half drawn back in a long tail secured with a black ribbon.

His warm hand covered hers at his elbow as they wandered the foyer and solar. They waited their turn to explore the marble cave set at the foot of the grand staircase, and Carys marveled at the shrine to Pythia, as well as all the other tributes to music and arts. She smiled at faces she recognized and especially those she almost did.

"Wolfgang would be mortified to see what they did to his nose," Carys whispered to her mate as they studied a golden bust of the small, energetic composer.

Gavriel's lips twitched, holding in his laugh.

Soon it was time to ascend the stairs, and Carys couldn't help comparing the marbles to her own coloring, a little habit she had.

"Yours is the more beautiful, you vain thing," Gavriel teased.

She batted her eyes at him as they entered the grand foyer. Following their fellow patrons, they strolled down the long hall, the floors gleaming under the low-hanging chandeliers. Statues of muses and famous composers stood to greet them along the way, their faces and limbs supple though carved from stone.

One caught her eye, and she dug her claws into the soft wool of Gavriel's sleeve.

They couldn't stop to look long, humans coming up behind them to get to their seats, but Carys would know that arch of horns anywhere.

"You're sure?" Gavriel murmured.

"Yes." She smiled up at him, already jubilant though the opening notes hadn't yet been played. They would have to figure out how to secret away a whole statue from a very public place, but that was a problem for tomorrow.

They found their seats, in a third-level box set back from the stage.

An older couple in finery that'd been fashionable fifteen years previous sat in the first seats, the woman's heavy perfume almost cloying. The woman looked at Carys's red gown and sniffed. Two other couples noted their arrival, the gentlemen nodding and the women noting the breadth of Gavriel's shoulders.

She and Gavriel shared a grin as they settled in. With the seats in the back row, Carys could unfold her wings more comfortably and not worry about her tail being trodden on. As the orchestra warmed up and more patrons filed into the auditorium below, Gavriel laid his hand in her lap and observed the humans, one of his favorite pastimes, while Carys idly toyed with his fingers.

In the ebbs and flows of their life, there were times they spent decades apart from the mortal world, ensconced at Caer Gwyn or Hillcrest. Being immersed in human society again took getting used to, and she was glad of a quiet moment to regain her bearings.

Carys had come to find that memory worked in interesting ways for those as long-lived as the fae. When she tried to recall something from hundreds of years past, she usually could, but there were still great swathes of time she'd simply forgotten. Perhaps it was that there just wasn't space enough in her memory and heart to keep everything. She remembered great events; could recall the sound of her clan singing and the sting of her mother's acerbic tongue, could remember tending the wounded of the many battlefields of Glyndwr's rebellion as well as touring Titian's workshop in Venice. She remembered dear human friends, like Alys and Mrs. Sully, and her most favorite animals.

Especially with the advent of printing and news passing more freely amongst humans, they had taken to retreating from society, allowing the memories of Lord and Lady Gwynvael to fade. After a time at Caer Gwyn or Hillcrest, they travelled to a new place to search out new leads. Before their last stay at Hillcrest, they'd spent three years in New York and found a good number of artifacts and statues. Before that had been Egypt, one of Carys's favorite places, though Gavriel wasn't fond of how his fine fae skin always sunburned.

She thought perhaps it was these flows, these retreats and reentries, and how her own mind had to cope with their longevity, that whenever she was around crowds of humans again, it took her a long while to relearn how to manage. She had to tuck her wings and watch her manners.

The past centuries had been perhaps a bit more difficult each time they returned. Carys could still remember when humans faced the dangers of the wilds, their villages small and their lifespans tragically short. There were so many of them now, spread across the globe, especially in their bustling cities that still astonished her with their sprawling enormity.

She sometimes worried how she and Gavriel would be able to continue hiding.

Gavriel squeezed her thigh as if sensing her whirring thoughts, and she looked up from her lap to realize that the opera was about to begin.

She caught his worried look from the corner of her eye and shook her head before resting it on his shoulder. She sighed, happy to put away her thoughts for a while. Tonight was for beautiful music and reuniting with another of her kin.

Soft violin notes wafted through the auditorium as patrons began to find their seats again after an intermission. Carys hummed, happy in her light doze against her mate's strong shoulder. The tip of her tail swung lazily in time with the little tune one of the musicians played as humans milled about.

Gavriel pressed his lips to her forehead. "I think they're starting again," he whispered into her hair.

Blinking awake, Carys watched the audience grow as humans returned from the foyer and vestibule. The violinist finished their song, and the buzz of excitement grew as seats were taken and music—

A violent *snap* echoed across the auditorium, followed immediately by an ominous creak that grated against her bones.

Gavriel's hand in her lap tensed, and he leaned forward in his seat, shielding her with his body.

The lights from the chandelier flickered. The towering bronze and crystal swayed, and in the next heartbeat, the chandelier careened to the auditorium floor below.

The audience gasped, the chandelier swooping down like a meteor, crashing into the second level balcony. Crystal shattered and women screamed as candles and shards rained down on the first level seats.

Springing from his seat, Gavriel leapt to the parapet with the other men to see. His hand flicked at his side, and all the chandelier candles went out.

There would be no fire at least.

Carys joined him at the balcony, and he tucked her into his side. They watched on with concern as others rallied to help clear crystal and cables. Several were pulled from under the pile, and the first level audience was hurried out through side doors. Not many had been in their seats thank the goddesses, and in the end, only one man was seriously hurt.

When a concierge came to usher them out, too, the other couples in the box went quickly, hands clutched to chests and already whispering over what they had seen.

Gavriel held her back, finding them a little recess in their box to stand in. He untied a red velvet curtain, obscuring them from the auditorium below, and settled in to wait, his arm slung around her waist to hold her back to his front.

"Unexpected, but we can use the distraction," he said.

She craned her neck to glare at him. "You didn't."

He stared back blandly. "Of course not. It's a bit too dramatic for me."

"Hmph."

They waited for long minutes as the sounds of workers and other opera house staff arrived to make sense of what happened. Colorful insults bandied about to the accompaniment of tinkling crystal. All the while, Gavriel traced patterns along her silk-clad middle, never straying too far up or down, just enough to let her know he was amenable.

It certainly wouldn't be the first time they had done wicked things in opulent public places. Or second. Or third.

Still, she was rattled by the crash and wanted to see this done. They may never have a better time to secret away her kin.

"I am disappointed we won't know what happens. With the opera," she whispered.

Gavriel chuckled and kissed the hollow behind her ear. "The Italians are fond of their melodrama. I'm sure at least one soprano has a tragic end."

She hummed in agreement. "The melodrama is what makes it so wonderful."

"Is your life lacking drama, Lady Gwynvael?"

"Sometimes. And that's how I prefer it. Though I will say, crashing chandeliers is quite enough for one night."

They waited another handful of minutes before venturing out from behind the curtain. Gavriel opened the door to the hallway and nodded for her to follow. They met no one in the hall, and in a stroke of luck, found the foyer deserted as well.

Hurrying to the statue they wanted, Carys took a moment to look the guardian over.

He was a handsome male, lithe for her kind, with arching horns and a shout on his lips. He'd been frozen in stone in the middle of a crouch, as if about to spring into the air or at an enemy. She reached out and touched the male's arm, and like with all her kin, she swore the stone was slightly warm under her palm.

"Let's take him home."

They took their positions, a practiced routine they'd perfected over the centuries. On Gavriel's count, they lifted the guardian off the floor. Her arms trembled with the effort, but they only needed it aloft by an inch.

Secured between them, Gavriel folded the realm around them, transporting all three back to their chateau outside the city.

They let the statue drop, safe in their home, and Carys took a step back to check the male over. Seeing he was no worse for wear from the quick trip, she took Gavriel's offered hand and the two transported back to the Palais Garnier.

All of it took mere moments.

Carys had caught her breath by the time they made it to the end of the Grand Foyer, where they were finally intercepted by an attendant.

"Please, *monsieur, madame*, this way," the young man said, ushering them out to the staircase.

They joined the other patrons lingering in the vestibule but skirted those harassing the staff for their money back.

"I don't know why they bother," noted Gavriel, "they certainly got their money's worth."

"As if this won't be all they speak about for a month," she agreed.

Walking arm in arm, they slipped hands into gloves as they exited, leaving behind the drama of the opera. A temperate Parisian night greeted them, and Carys drew in a long breath of it. Roses bloomed nearby, and the smells of the fine restaurants tempted in hungry patrons.

"It'd be a shame to waste the evening and that dress," Gavriel said.

"Indeed," she replied, straightening the silk rose pinned in her hair. "I suppose I could allow you to buy me dinner."

"Anything, *cariad*. You know that."

VII

His lieutenant took the steep, winding road up to the castle like the racecar driver he'd been before the war, tires squealing and dust flying. An *oof* emanated from the backseat, the two corporals smashed together as they rounded the last hairpin turn up to the castle gatehouse.

Gavriel shot an unamused look at Barnes, his devil-may-care lieutenant with a death wish, but the Welshman just grinned cockily. They sped into the front courtyard well ahead of the other trucks carrying the rest of their small unit, the unfortunate corporals groaning in relief as they came to a stop.

"In one piece, as promised, captain," Barnes said, fishing a cigarette out of his front pocket.

"That remains to be seen," Gavriel replied as the corporals spilled out of the truck, one hustling to the castle wall to wretch into the forest below.

Exiting the truck, Gavriel straightened his jacket and donned his hat.

Before them, Neuschwanstein Castle in all its fairytale beauty reached to the sky, white walls and blue rooves and turrets gleaming. He'd only heard stories of the place and its pseudo-Gothic extravagance; he and his mate hadn't visited the Prussian states in a long while. He could admit, it was a lovely building; dominating the valley, it stood above in nostalgic elegance and bygone beauty. He'd seen the Gothic castles it was built to resemble before they crumbled away to history and decided it was a pretty facsimile.

But he wasn't here for the fairy castle, nor really the treasures hidden here by their Nazi enemies. He was after something far more precious.

Turning to Barnes, Gavriel said, "Have the men assemble. I'll find Captain Rorimer to see what use he has for us. I expect we'll rejoin the Fifty-Third in a few days."

Barnes gave him a two-fingered salute and sauntered off to meet the rest of their unit, still ambling up the road. They weren't strictly needed here; orders hadn't come from above, so Gavriel kept the unit small and the jaunt short. He couldn't resist coming, though, that hadn't been an option.

After the hell he and his men had endured taking the Reichswald, he needed to see her.

Gavriel made his way up the stairs to the entrance, barred by polished wood and wrought-iron doors. Using his shoulder, he opened one to a sumptuous display of color. Rich reds, blues, and golds saturated the lower hall, the frescoes almost as alive as the men moving about the space. Some carried delicate artworks by their ornate frames, others had boxes of silver or whole tureens cradled in their arms. Yet more held documents or took notes.

All through the hall, a buzz of excited work echoed to the rafters.

How extraordinary it must have been for these men, just a few days before finding this out-of-the-way castle, the pet project of a mad king hoarding another pet project of a far more dangerous madman, filled to the brim with stolen treasure.

A glint of golden hair caught his eye, and Gavriel cut through the hall, passing over other Monuments Men to instead approach a pair discussing an enormous set of silver platters.

"Gentlemen."

The men turned at his greeting. One was a tall man, middle-aged, with receding hair and round spectacles. The other was shorter, more youthful, with a head of short blonde curls and a vaguely familiar face tucked under an officer's hat.

"Captain Gilbert Gwyneth, Fifty-Third Infantry. I'm looking for Captain Rorimer."

"He should be up in the Hall of Singers. I'll take you there," said the blonde man.

"Much obliged."

The bespectacled man shrugged and went back to surveying the platters, leaving Gavriel to follow the shorter man.

The soldier led him deeper into the palace, inside richly decorated rooms that looked spun from pure fantasies of medieval days. Ornately carved woods, saturated greens and reds, animal motifs—they all vaguely reminded him of the halls he and his mate had visited back then.

Gavriel's magick hummed inside him, little sparks dancing from his fingertips that kept tempo with his quickening pulse. With every step, the glamour concealing the man walking in front of him melted away, revealing long tresses of golden curls, pink marble wings, and a supple backside that haunted his dreams.

He barely saw the rooms they strode through, his legs eating the distance as her pace hastened from walk to almost a jog. She took a sharp right through an open arched door and pulled him in behind her.

It was a circular stone room, in one of the turret towers, and empty of anything else.

Good. Because he couldn't wait any longer.

"Hello, captain," she said, closed and latched door at her back. Her coin-gold eyes shone from the morning light filtering in through the windows.

"Hello, *cariad*," he said, tipping up her hat to let the brim rest jauntily on her little horns.

Carys smiled, showing off her pretty little fangs. She held her ground as he closed the distance between them, chin tilting up to keep his hungry gaze.

"Shouldn't you be in Berlin?"

"Soon enough. I had to see you."

The playful smile fell, and in the next moment, she was in his arms finally, where she belonged.

Their hats went sailing to the stone floor as their lips met in a violent clash, a desperate declaration that they were both here, together, alive. They'd spent months, sometimes even years apart before; his predilection to wander could get the better of him or one of them wanted to stay on longer somewhere on their journeys. The time apart could be good, renewing—but it always proved to him, time and again, that being together, with her, was best.

This last separation had been different. Though they usually stayed out of human affairs, the conflicts of this century had pulled everything into their orbit, including the two of them. In the Great War, they'd both served as field doctors, patching men up in triage. They could work longer and were immune to the diseases that plagued the field hospitals. After years of blown apart boys with lungs scalded by gas, they'd hoped to never witness such atrocity again.

They'd been at their chateau outside Paris when the opening volleys fired across Poland. When the Nazis came for France, they'd moved everything from their home to the safety of Caer Gwyn. But Carys had returned to help the French Resistance, and Gavriel had enlisted with the Royal Air Force. For a year he spent his nights dancing with enemy pilots over London, defending the Green Isle.

They'd seen each other when they could, Gavriel folding space around him when he knew where she'd be. After the landing at Normandy, she'd taken up with the Monuments, Fine Arts, and Archives program, eager to recover stolen treasures and ensure that none of her kin were among them. Gavriel had taken a captainship with the 53rd Welsh Division, cutting through occupied France and finally the Rhineland.

Those months of battle in the German forests had been brutal. For all the new, horrible ways humans had to kill one another, the fighting in many places had been with fists and bayonets and knives—like ancient battles that were decided with sword and axe. It was a horrid way to die and to kill.

The *rat-a-tat* of machine guns and *booms* of grenades, the hollow screams from bombed-out foxholes and squelch of the spring mud even now rang in Gavriel's ears, and he buried his face in the crook of his mate's neck.

He shuddered as she raked a clawed hand gently through his hair.

"*Fy annwyl*," she crooned.

"How I've missed you."

"Just a little bit longer."

"I know. But I couldn't wait. Never again." He raised his head, eyes bright with unshed tears. "After this, we go home and we stay in bed for days. And we don't part for more than a day. Never again."

"Never," she promised.

His mouth found hers again, hungry for her softness and promises. She nipped his lip with her fangs, making him growl. He devoured her sharp inhale, his magick sparking around them as he filled his hands with her backside and lifted her.

She flung her legs around him, moaning when he set her against the wall and leaned his weight into her. He could feel the heat of her reaching out to the searing bar of his cock even through their trousers.

His hands held her up, but he pooled his magick around her, let her feel its ethereal, insubstantial weight. It dripped down her neck and chest like warm syrup, flowing down to her breasts were it circled her pert nipples.

Carys gasped, head thrown back, and Gavriel dove for her neck, kissing and licking and nipping the column of her throat.

He felt her fervent little claws working their zippers, and he hissed when she filled her palm with his cock and pumped.

"Put me inside you," he growled against her lips.

With a needy hum, she adjusted her grip, ran him through her slick once, twice, and then notched him at her entrance. He couldn't wait, pushing inside, filling her up in one sure, relentless thrust.

Her mouth fell open in a silent cry, claws digging into his shoulders. Gavriel let his magick gush down to where their bodies met, pooling it against her sensitive clit.

"Gav-ri-el," she whined.

"How you burn for me, *cariad*," he groaned, fingers digging into her soft flank.

She bounced on his cock, the wet slap of their bodies muffled slightly by their uniforms. Nothing could contain her moans and mewls of pleasure, and Gavriel claimed it all like the greedy male he was, sucking on her lower lip, the rapid pulse at her throat, the hard point of her nipple through her jacket.

His hips rolled like the crashing tide, a flood of lust and desperation and relief. He gave her all of it, hips pistoning, spearing inside to claim all of her.

With a shout, Carys came, claws tangled in his hair. He pushed off from the wall, holding her aloft, and brought her down on his cock again, again, again—

Gavriel threw his head back and roared, filling his mate up to the brim. The pressure at his lower back crescendoed, releasing with a pleasure that bordered on pain. His thrusts slowed in tempo, though his hips couldn't quite stop, the delicious drag in and out of her too addicting.

"Ah, *cariad*," he sighed. His magick helped hold her steady as he sank to the ground, laying on his back with her cradled on his chest.

They lay like that for a long while, light from one of the windows puddling across them and making the gold veins in her skin sparkle.

He traced lazy patterns across the delicate membrane of her wings, wishing they could be fully skin to skin. He wished with a fervency close to pain to be at Caer Gwyn, in the bed he'd carved for her three hundred years ago, surrounded by their things and their life together.

But he knew his men, human and mortal, longed for the very same things and so couldn't abandon them even for a night, couldn't go home when they couldn't.

Perhaps she sensed the dour turn to his thoughts, for Carys lifted from her comfortable place on his chest to slowly unbutton his jacket. "Tell me," she said as she worked on his shirt.

Drawing in a long breath, he filled his palms with her hips and told her quietly of the spring offensive, how hard the fighting had been for the forests. He spoke of his men's grief and his own, too, of the horrors they'd seen and done.

She pressed soft kisses to his face, neck, and chest as he spoke, and her gentleness, as it always did, soothed those hurt parts of him that only she saw.

When he finished, she kissed him. "You were so brave, all of you. War is ugly, but you got your men through it. That's all you can do." And she kissed him again to seal her words inside him.

Once he was drunk on her kisses and compassion, she reached between them to guide his cock back inside her. She worked herself over him in little rocking bounces until she sat astride him.

Gavriel's breath shuddered through him watching her, seeing her stretched wide around him, the little pearl of her clit peeking between her folds. She petted his chest and gently clenched around him, milking his cock, and he nearly choked.

Gritting his teeth, he kept his hold gentle, determined to watch and see and enjoy.

Smiling down at him, a little of that playfulness returned to her expression. She slowly unbuttoned her own jacket then her shirt except the last two buttons. She pulled the gaping fabric back to reveal her large breasts, dusky pink nipples pouting and teasing him. Shirt held back by the bounty of her breasts, she teased her fingers over her nipples in little flutters before filling her palms.

His *cariad* knew just what he needed and liked and gave it to him.

She played with herself as she rocked slowly on him. Bathed in sunlight, she was more beautiful than all the treasures hidden away here. Resplendent, powerful, sexy.

His mate rode him at her leisure and all he could do was hang on.

He let his fingers stray over where they joined, slippery with their slick. His thumb found her clit, and he circled it in time to her gentle rhythm. She hummed in pleasure, and he felt it everywhere, but especially all around his cock.

Her pace began to quicken, and so too did Gavriel's circles. He rolled her clit between the pad of his thumb and hardness of his cock, making her whimper. When he added a gentle caress of magick to her wing bases and the undersides of her breasts, her hips snapped down.

It came much more gently this time, his pleasure peaking in a way that filled him up as surely as he filled his mate. He rolled his hips, meeting her rhythm and making those glorious breasts bounce, drawing out the orgasm so it could last him. It swept them both up in its current, stretching for long moments that he wished could last longer.

Thoroughly spent, Carys melted into his chest, head finding the dip between his pectorals that fit her perfectly. He tangled his fingers in her wild hair and stroked light fingertips up and down her leg. She sighed happily, and then they were quiet for a long while.

He could almost have dozed, but eventually Carys asked, "Won't your men be missing you?"

"Likely."

"Then come on. I have something to show you."

"I've already seen what I came for." He palmed her breasts and squeezed.

She guffawed in mock-offense, smacking at his hands. "Button your shirt, soldier. We have business."

Soul a little lighter, Gavriel finally rose from the floor. They buttoned each other back into shirts and jackets, and he placed the hat back on her head, brim balanced on her horns.

"I like the hat," he quipped.

"I'll keep it on next time," she said with a wink, darting out of the room before he could grab her.

He followed her into the corridor and through more lavishly styled rooms. They ascended a set of stairs up to the fourth level, but rather than leading him into the grand Hall of Singers, Carys pulled him into a smaller room nearby.

Inside was full to bursting with statuary.

And standing against the east wall, backlit by the sun, stood at least a half-dozen guardian statues.

"You found them," he marveled with a smile.

Carys grinned ear to ear, bouncing to her kin. She held the hand of a female, and Gavriel realized that this statue was unlike others they'd found. Two guardians had been locked together in stone, obviously a pair, with the female crouched to pull at something at her thigh and the male standing over her protectively.

"This is my sister."

Gavriel blinked, not quite understanding. Over the years, his mate had come to refer to the statues as her brothers and sisters, and at first, he thought that was what she meant.

But her smile grew watery, and the way she touched the female statue's arm had him realizing . . .

"Oh, *fy annwyl.*" He closed the space between them and wrapped her in his arms. Kissing the top of her head, he said, "We'll finally bring her home."

"I thought she'd been destroyed. I'd begun to lose hope."

"You found her. You've done it, *cariad.*"

With this new group, they had almost two-hundred guardians stored safely at Caer Gwyn. He didn't know why, but it felt significant to have so many. Carys didn't think there could be many more, between the guardians' numbers when Titania cursed them and the intervening millennia.

Perhaps, all together . . .

Gavriel looked about the room, at all the other statuary gathered there. So many treasures kept here, and rumor was that this was only the start, that much more had been spirited away before the Allies could secure the region.

So much treasure, so much history.

He and Carys had gathered their own collection over the centuries, not just the guardians. And while the Nazis and their grand designs of a museum full of the best European art, plundered from the nations they'd razed, was laughable to him, it did make him think.

He hadn't forgotten his theory that the mate bond could be what helped break this curse. If not an answer then at least a start.

But if they had all the guardians there were to have together, including a mated pair fused together already in stone, and none roused another, then perhaps it was humans who could stir this mate bond. Carys had spoken before that it could happen between her kind and humans, had on rare occasions between guardians and Pritani.

They'd tried it once to small crowds of nosy elites, and Gavriel wasn't keen on having people traipsing through his home again. After this, their home was for them and he wanted to stay there for a good decade.

But after . . . if they could display their collection . . .

"*Cariad*, I have an idea . . ."

VIII

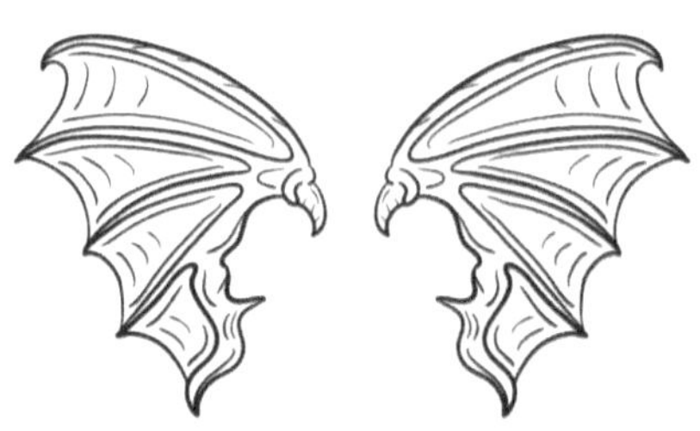

Present Day
Caer Gwyn, Cymru (Wales)

Music blared from the sound system as Carys scrubbed dishes in the sink, sleeves pushed up to her elbows and tail bouncing to the rhythm. She'd worn out the dogs with her antics and the cats had never been interested, so she sang and danced on her own, wiling away the lonely hours with housework.

It was late into the night, yet she couldn't sleep. Rather than even trying, she'd busied herself all day, trying to tucker herself out.

Waiting for his call.

There'd been disappointingly little to clean in the kitchen. Gavriel kept it pristine, every surface gleaming, every knife and pot stored exactly where it was meant. They'd kitted out their kitchen with all the best modern appliances a few years ago. Gavriel had always been an excellent cook, but once he discovered his love of charcuterie, he needed a kitchen to match.

Their home had gone through many changes over the years. To add warmth and a touch of the modern, they'd made the kitchen and the large den adjoining it the center hub of the home. They'd had to knock out a wall to build the den and filled the new room with overstuffed couches, a palatial fireplace and stone mantel, a low table piled with photography books, and built-in shelves on the north and west walls.

The original stone of their home blended with the new wood and fabrics they'd brought in over the centuries. Other parts of the home remained in the past, and for the most part, they enjoyed it that way. The magick that imbued their land and the house had a way of keeping their treasures safe and preserved, so as long as it was treated with care, many of their pieces looked as fine as when they'd first found them.

Their library was full to bursting with rare tomes and penny-dreadfuls, globes with borders that no longer existed, Persian rugs, Victorian desks and Baroque chairs, spyglasses and telescopes and sextants, medieval tapestries and art nouveau lamps. Her personal solar still held many of her most precious things from her life and travels, favorite dresses and fabrics, books, art, and a little vase collection she'd started in the 17th century just because she could.

So much of their home told the stories of the centuries it and they had lived; it was nice to have a room that was modern.

Especially the microwave, though Gavriel would shudder in horror to know she'd reheated takeaway for dinner.

But takeaway meant little to clean up afterwards. So, dozens of cookies, dog biscuits, and cupcakes later, Carys was happily cleaning up her baking mess. She chuckled evilly to herself thinking of her mate's face when he saw what an adventure she'd had in his kitchen. She'd leave it spotless, and he'd smile that tight smile and nod, but he'd clean it himself when he thought she was asleep.

Carys was just drying her hands on a dishcloth when the dramatic organ music from the seminal song of *The Phantom of the Opera* blared across the living room. She dashed around the kitchen island and dove over the den couch for her phone, giggling at her own joke. Gavriel always just rolled his eyes at her ringtone for him, but she enjoyed it to no end.

Accepting the video call, her mate's handsome face took over the screen.

"Hello, *cariad*," he said, looking far too delectable in a gray fisherman sweater that clung to his strong form. She almost regretted buying it for him, it looked far too good and made her far too amenable to whatever suggestions he made while wearing it.

Her toes curled hearing his deep, lyrical purr. He'd only been gone about twenty hours, on a red-eye flight from London to San Francisco, but she already missed him.

Since the war, they'd been good to their word—no more than a night apart.

"Hello, *fy nghariad*," she said, swinging her legs from where they dangled over the couch. "How was the flight?"

Her mate loved flying, had caught the bug during his service in the Royal Air Force. He said it was much more pleasant to fly in the daylight, without being shot at. A marvel too that they could step into an airplane and be anywhere in the world in a day or two.

With so many humans and the advent of technology—especially cameras—it wasn't safe for Gavriel to fold the realm around him unless it was to come home. Yes, he'd been many places before and therefore could easily bend the realm and step into the Louvre or onto the Great Wall of China, but he'd do it in front of dozens if not hundreds of humans, all with their phone cameras out.

At least with air travel, he could still go wandering and transport himself home. They saved a fortune on airfare.

"Easy enough, we got in early. I had time before the meeting, so I walked down to the wharves. The weather is moody here, fog and clouds and sunshine and wind all in a day. You'll love it."

She did always like dramatic weather.

"So you liked the building, I take it?"

Gavriel dangled a set of keys and fobs in front of his camera and jangled them. "There's a bit more paperwork to be done, but it's ours."

Carys laughed. "That was fast."

"The location is excellent and it will suit us nicely." The keys vanished so that he could claim the whole screen with his wicked smile. "Besides, if I was to be apart from you, I might as well make it worth it."

"Well, let's see this building you bought without even asking your mate."

He winked and turned the camera to face out. It was late afternoon in California, and thick rays of sun slanted into the front of the building through walls of glass. From behind the camera, Gavriel led her on a tour, showing her the spacious lobby, which already included a front desk and water feature, then down a wide corridor punctuated by recessed alcoves.

"Apparently the last tenant was some sort of marketing company, but the owner liked art." He moved the camera to show her the alcoves, complete with pediments and backlights, ready to show off a statue.

"And here is the *coup de gras*."

Through a cased opening, the corridor spilled into a grand three-story hall, the airy space lit by a peaked roof of glass. Breezy galleries on the second and third floors opened up into the space on the east and west walls. The marble floors of the central aisle gleamed under the bright daylight, and canned recess lights added a warm glow.

It took Carys's breath away, reminding her of a Byzantine basilica but made of iron and glass.

"There are more rooms upstairs and more alcoves, but I thought this would be the perfect place for some of your kin."

Carys smiled, nose almost touching her phone she held it so close to her face. The space was perfect, and she was already thinking of who could go where within the airy main room.

The camera flipped back around to show Gavriel with a small, hopeful smile. That he'd done this for her, wanting to please her, made her heart thump and his magick inside her purr in happiness.

"Do you like it, *fy annwyl?*" he asked. "I know nothing happened in London, but I have a good feeling about this. I can't describe it . . ."

This male. Her cheeks glowed pink with her blush, and she almost squirmed on the couch with love for him.

After the war, Gavriel had had the idea to exhibit their collection as a museum or gallery, to draw in humans and see if any of them might spark . . . something. His hunch about the mate bond was the first real strategy they'd had in centuries, and she was willing to try anything.

It ate at her sometimes, that they'd been unable to help even one of their peoples. For all the books and knowledge and wealth they'd amassed over more than a millennium, they had yet to put it to much use for their kin.

They'd tried their first gallery in London a few years before. She'd selected only a few guardian statues and filled the rest of the collection with other interesting, beautiful things. The launch had gone well, attracting thousands of visitors, and her hopes had been high. Yet, nothing happened, and when a handful of academics from the British Museum came sniffing, whispering about provenance under their breath, she and Gavriel decided it was time to take the collection and try their luck elsewhere.

When Gavriel suggested trying the American west coast, she'd been amenable. Why not. They'd never spent much time there, had stuck to the more established east, where they were more likely to find statues and other precious things.

Seeing the building he'd chosen for their new gallery, Carys felt that same spark of . . . *something* bursting inside her. She was too old now for optimism, but all they could do was try.

"I love it," she said, humming with fresh excitement.

His brow arched, and from the way his image moved slightly, she knew he shifted his weight from one foot to the other. She knew too what he'd say before he said it, yet still grinned and squirmed when he asked, "And do you think this warrants a boon?"

"What about not being scolded for buying a building without me?"

"Hmm," he hummed, making her squirm again deeper into the couch. She bit the claw of a finger and gave him a grin full of fang.

She'd long since given up being embarrassed by how attracted she was to her mate. It was in a guardian's nature to adore their heartsong, but there were times over the centuries she'd wondered if she might grow a little more immune to his charms. They'd lived long enough to have tried almost everything that interested them—they attended bacchanals and orgies, used toys and aphrodisiacs, role swapped and roleplayed. They'd made love in every room, on every surface of every home they owned, had had sex in castles and forests and libraries and sitting rooms. They'd spent days wallowing in pleasure, claimed quickies in hidden niches, and everything in between.

There were some days that just being with him was enough, and there had been decades they spent more time apart than together pursuing their own interests. But after the World Wars and the atrocities of them, it was almost like those first years of matehood all over again, when intimacy was a daily ritual.

She'd come to crave it again, and even now, she felt herself warming and readying for him.

And he knew it. Thousands of miles away, he knew.

"What do you want as a boon?" she asked, giving in because his boons were almost always boons for her as well.

His smile was languid, showing off the tips of his own fangs. He took his time running his eyes over everything of her he could see, gaze sultry under heavy lids and long lashes. She'd always found his long, sooty lashes wholly unfair.

The breath he drew as he considered was long and deep and completely for show. She could tell from the satisfied grin tugging at his lips that he already knew exactly what he wanted.

"What are you wearing, *cariad?*"

She held the phone away from her to show off her oversized sweater and tight leggings.

A rumble of pleasure reverberated from his throat. "Leggings are my favorite modern garment."

Because they left nothing of the shape of her legs to the imagination. She enjoyed the lightweight fit and comfort; Gavriel enjoyed all her curves on display and how easy they were to peel off.

That didn't stop him, though, from requesting she wear one of her old frocks when they played in their woods outside Caer Gwyn or Hillcrest. There was something more exciting about running from and being caught by a forest spirit in petticoats. For all that he enjoyed the accessibility afforded by modern clothes, her mate still loved revealing her under all those frothy skirts to his hungry gaze.

His gaze was positively ravenous now, and her breaths quickened when he rumbled, "Put your phone on the table so I can see you."

Swallowing on a dry throat, Carys propped her phone against a stack of photobooks, leaving her hands free.

"Take your leggings off. Panties, too."

"I'm not wearing any," she told the screen before standing up. His appreciative groan spurred her to make it a little show for him, turning around to wiggle her backside as she slipped out of the leggings. She bit her lip around a smile as she bent over to step out of the clingy fabric and heard him groan again.

"Sit back on the couch," he said thickly.

She took her time, easing down onto the cushions and shivering at the delicious slide of warm leather against her bare bottom. Finding a comfortable position for her wings, she let the couch cradle her and waited with bated breath for her mate to continue.

They'd seen many new inventions through the years and taken an interest in the burgeoning technology of the last century. Photography interested them early on, as did genetics and steam engines and automobiles. They both enjoyed gramophones and records and always invested in sound systems to fill their homes with music. Neither of them had quite taken to television programs, but they did enjoy movies and both had a plethora of YouTube hobbyists they followed.

But her favorite thing was smartphones—particularly the cameras. And all her game apps, if she was honest. The camera meant at least being able to see each other, and they'd discovered many new . . . tantalizing aspects of the digital age.

"Unbutton your sweater."

Her deft claws could make quick work of it, but that wasn't part of the fun. She took her time, watching as his camera shifted with his weight from foot to foot.

With the last button free, she opened the soft cashmere to reveal her lacy bra. Pink with embroidered flowers and lace trim, it was a favorite for both of them. Gavriel's eyes sparkled like diamonds to see it.

"Just look at you, *cariad*. So pretty and waiting for me. Show me where you need me."

A happy sigh on her lips, she leaned back into the couch and slowly dragged her claws down her body. His quicksilver eyes watched it all, unblinking gaze hungry and intense. When her fingers reached her mons, she shifted her legs apart, revealing her warm core.

"*Ffyc*," he groaned, "show me, *cariad*."

Blushing and aroused, she hooked an arm on the back of the couch, arching her back and pushing out her breasts, as her other hand ran down through her slick and back up again, parting her folds to show off all her pink flesh.

"That's good. Just like that, *fy annwyl*. Hold still for me."

It was just a brush at first, a warm caress she felt along the tops of her thighs. She shuddered in delight as his magick moved up her legs, the effervescent wisps barely visible, like heat rising from baked earth.

Through many such calls, they'd discovered he could still use his magick through the phone. It wasn't as strong as when he was there with her, diluted by distance, but so long as he could see her, he could use his magick to stroke and caress and fuck her.

His magick pressed warmly against her, surrounding her fingers and clit, an insubstantial but insistent pressure. Tendrils wound up her middle in fleeting little caresses until they reached her bra. With the smallest tug, his magick pulled the cups down enough for her nipples to spill free. Carys squirmed as his magick lapped at her and rolled her nipples against the satiny brims.

"Hold still," he rasped, and with a plaintive moan, she stilled. "Good girl."

His magick swirled around her clit, never giving enough pressure, then slid down to her entrance. She felt the warm slide of it, delving inside. Not quite like his fingers or tongue or cock, it was just enough to tease, shallow thrusts that made her writhe.

Her head thrashed on the cushion, and her hand trembled keeping herself open to him. She'd barely have to move her fingers to give herself the pressure she craved, but she wanted him to do it, wanted to see what he'd do next.

Her mouth fell open on a gasp when more magick teased her opening, enough to stretch her as if it was his cock. Warmth gushed from her, and nonsensical sounds spilled from her lips.

Unable to stop, her hips rolled with his magick's rhythm.

"*Ffyc, cariad.* Stay just like that."

Suddenly, everything stopped. His magick vanished, and she clenched around emptiness with a whimper.

From the corner of her eye, she saw the living room bend and contort. A rip rent through the room, and from the nebulous colors of in between, her mate stepped. It winked out as quickly as it formed, Gavriel stalking toward her.

He tossed his phone on the table beside hers and gazed down at her, needy and wanting.

Shoulders tense, he was a predator about to pounce, waiting for the perfect opportunity. His muscles bunched under the thick sweater, and an insistent bulge pressed against the seam of his tailored trousers.

He inhaled sharply before letting a maddeningly smug smile overcome his face.

His magick grasped her ankles, stronger than before, almost as firm and warm as his hands. It was a sense of weight and pressure, one she could break free of whenever she wanted, but instead let it pull her to the end of the couch and set her legs apart, one over the back and one over the arm.

Gavriel watched as his magick arranged her to his liking, unhurried as he undressed. First went his belt then his shoes. He pulled his sweater over his head and bunched it under her head. Then went his trousers, until he stood naked at the side of the couch, looming above her as his magick kept her still.

He hummed in appreciation, stepping between her legs to run his hands up her thighs.

"You always know how to welcome me home, sweetling."

Carys threw her head back on a cry of pleasure when his fingers finally found her clit. His magick was divine, but it couldn't imitate the rasp of his calluses or the pressure of knuckles. Still, it had her writhing when the magick slipped back up her chest to cup her breasts beneath the bra, swirling around her nipples.

He kept her like that for a long while, spread wide for his pleasure as he pushed her almost past the point of sanity. Two fingers took up where his magick had left off, gently thrusting inside. He watched his fingers disappear inside her, gaze rapt as he curled those fingers against the spot inside he liked to toy with. Her back bowed, orgasm nearly cresting—

Only for him to pull out and begin circling her clit again.

Growling, Carys scowled at him, which only made him chuckle.

"Patience, *cariad*. Won't it make the reunion sweeter?"

But as he played with and pleasured her again and again, teasing her to a peak only to deny her, she careened past wanting sweet.

She knew from experience he could keep her like this for hours, days even. They'd spent many days torturing each other with pleasure just for the sake of it. She'd gone through days with his magick always there, inside her, slowly thrusting into her as she attempted to do chores. Always on the edge, always about to fly.

Perhaps it was him being fae; so long-lived, she'd come to find that fae were rarely rushed. He didn't consider it going slow but taking his time, of which he had a plethora.

Perhaps she'd let him do that later, but right now, she wanted it too much.

Shifting her hips, she trailed the tip of her tail up his thigh. She felt him shudder under her teasing touches, and before he could nab it, she curled her tail around his cock and squeezed.

He nearly doubled over in a wheezing groan. She gentled her hold just a bit but kept hold of him, pumping slowly and teasing the wet slit on the broad head with the tip of her tail.

"Insatiable wench," he choked.

She could only moan in response, beyond words. His fingers held her open as she guided him inside, and when he was notched at her entrance, her tail fell away. Though she did swat his backside for good measure.

He worked himself deeper in controlled thrusts, hands at her thighs to keep her flush and open to his invasion.

She pulled her bra down to knead her breasts, but felt his magick weaving between her fingers.

"Hands above your head."

On a groan she complied, laying her hands back on the couch cushions. His magick instead played with her breasts, plumping and kneading and rolling.

"Look at you, *cariad*, all open for me."

Finally, with a brutal thrust, he pushed all the way inside. He set them a hard pace, flesh slapping wetly and her breasts bouncing as he worked her on his cock. Her head thrashed back and forth as her orgasm ripped through her, walls clutching at him. It rolled from one to the next, never-ending, her entire body a sensitive, exposed nerve that could only take and feel.

The part of his magick inside her thrummed happily, keeping tempo to her thundering heart and his hammering hips. She felt as if she'd burst from her skin, so full of magick and happiness and him.

With a roar, Gavriel came, grinding his pelvis down on hers to send her flying again. His hips lost their rhythm, thrusts gone jerky as he filled her again and again. He moaned her name before easing down to her, giving her his weight.

It wasn't for what felt like a long while that she could find the strength to move. Still trembling from the onslaught of pleasure, she traced the long point of her mate's ear, toying with the silver hoops.

Gavriel lifted his head, kissed between her breasts, and straightened. In efficient movements, he cleaned them up and then set her back on the couch. She let him move her about, too comfortable to do it herself. He unhooked her bra and set it aside with her sweater, leaving her naked and laying on her back.

He settled himself into the cradle of her body, head pillowed on her chest. She tangled their legs together and ran her claws gently down his back, up his neck, into his curtain of silvery-blonde hair, and down again.

The house settled into peaceful somnolence, all soft breaths and warm touches. She dozed for a time, content with the reassuring weight of her mate so close to the heart that beat for him.

After a while, Gavriel murmured into her skin, "You really like the building?"

"Yes. It's perfect. It feels . . . right."

He lifted his head to prop his chin on her sternum.

"I've always believed that something brought us together. Something powerful, divine even. It can't have been just chance."

"Chance would be too simple."

Nothing about freeing their kin had been simple. She'd gathered as many guardians as she thought left in the world and still nothing. Gavriel kept a close eye on archaeological projects in the country as well as historical research conducted on the early history of Britain. They had performed rituals at the henges and made offerings every solstice. They had pieces, clues, but nothing that had led them to Morrígan or the Underhill or an answer to the guardians' curse.

"I have hope, though," he said.

"I know. I do, too. You give me hope."

His smile was small but precious, one she rarely saw. She knew he worried that while he could fulfill his duties as a mate and had provided her a good life, he'd failed to find a solution. She had her own worries that dogged her through the centuries, but he never let them discourage her, just as she never let him believe that he had or ever would fail her.

He leaned forward to kiss her tenderly. "I love you, *cariad*."

"And I love you, heartsong. Always."

If the centuries had taught her nothing else, Carys knew that she could face anything so long as her mate stood beside her. He gave her hope and strength. He was her constant in a changing world, so different from the one she'd once known.

She would always try to free their people, but he would always be first in her heart. If they truly couldn't free the guardians and the fae, if their mating truly was an aberration of chance, it wouldn't change anything.

Gavriel was nothing like what she'd imagined her mate would be, yet was everything she'd hoped he would be.

He was just . . . *everything*.

Within a handful of weeks, their plans for a museum had begun to take shape. Carys had already walked through the clan, telling them excitedly of the new development, how she hoped this would lead to something, and that at least a museum would make for more entertainment than the quiet idyll of Caer Gwyn.

Sorting what would be moved in first had been a task—one that'd taken days. All the bits and bobs they would display alongside the clan had to be carefully selected. And found. Carys wasn't too proud to admit that her cataloguing system left something to be desired, and it was only after a harrowing ordeal of digging through boxes, trunks, and spiderwebs that she was able to find everything she wanted to start filling the museum.

Then there were the small tiffs on how best to move and arrange the guardians. Even after centuries together, she and her fae still had strong opinions on the arrangement of statuary—and his opinions were more often wrong than hers.

Once a system was negotiated over a cutthroat game of whist one night, everything went smoother. They didn't trust anyone to handle their precious guardians and artefacts, so each piece and person was carefully transported from Caer Gwyn to the San Francisco location via portal. There, each was lovingly placed to its best effect.

Seeing the space fill up with her kin and the many things she and Gavriel had amassed over the centuries filled her with a sort of pride. There was something awe-inspiring to see the main gallery of the museum, boasting dozens of guardians. A conclave of them, each on their own pedestal to showcase their power and grace.

Like this, under the recessed lighting and painted alcoves, her kin almost looked alive.

Sooner than she could believe, it was time to begin interviewing for staff. They couldn't run an operation such as this by themselves— not to mention, doing so would look suspicious to the humans of San Francisco. So, they'd settled on hiring a small team of professionals.

"But only those who clearly love the collection," Carys stipulated. "The clan aren't just a job."

Gavriel grinned fondly. "Of course, *cariad*."

And that was how, on a bright California afternoon, Carys sat with her handsome mate in their new office, interviewing their first applicant.

They'd had many applications, but something about this one felt . . . special. She couldn't quite put her finger on what drew her to this Anna Kincaid. Even as just a name on paper, her attention had been snagged. Now, sitting across from the pleasant young woman, Carys felt the zinging energy of realms zip down her spine.

Gavriel reached out to squeeze her hands. *He feels it, too.*

Smiling, Carys leaned forward to greet the woman. "Tell us about yourself, Anna."

*The story continues with Heartsong,
available soon from Avon Books . . .*

Epilogue Notes

I

1. I've attempted to use place names as they would have been used to the people who lived there. Of course, as someone who doesn't speak Welsh and is just doing my best internet sleuthing, I'm sure I made mistakes, but I hope the overall effect worked!

2. The name for the land of Wales is Cymru and the Welsh people call themselves the Cymry. The word Wales, and therefore Welsh, derives through the grapevine of Old English, Proto-German, and Roman Latin as a word for inhabitants of the western territories of the Roman Empire. It is thought to originate from the Latin word for one of the Celtic tribes in Gaul (modern France). Over the centuries, it came to refer to Celtic Britons, particularly by the Anglo-Saxon ethnic groups ruling England. At first, it referred to all things the Saxons considered to be Briton and was not restricted to Wales—it could refer to Cornwall and other such non-Anglo-Saxon areas in Britain. Essentially, it was a way to refer to a different ethnic group in this volatile clash of Romano-Celtic and Anglo-Saxon culture.

In a similar vein, the region of Snowdonia in Wales, which today is a national park, is traditionally known of Eryri. There is a movement in Wales to officially reestablish its traditional name.

3. There is some debate over where exactly Pengwern was in early medieval Wales, though in general it's believed to be what is now considered northeastern Wales and parts of the English Midlands/ Marches. It also isn't fully understood how autonomous Pengwern was from the larger kingdom of Powys, especially as the latter absorbed some of what had been Pengwern upon its collapse. Its last ruler, Cynddylan, is a bit of a murky character and doesn't appear until later sources and stories, but the kingdom of Pengwern is believed to have existed at some point.

II

1. Gruffydd ap Llywelyn was the first king of what we would consider a unified Wales from 1055–1063. First king of Gwynedd and Powys, he conquered the other smaller petty kingdoms to the south to form a country not dissimilar to its neighboring England. Since the collapse of the Roman Empire and Roman rule in Britain, the Welsh petty kingdoms had fought one another as often as they did their Anglo-Saxon rivals to the east. Gruffydd was the first to control most of what new now consider Wales under central leadership. It was noted as a time of peace and unification. However, this would only last until his death in 1063. The kingdom was divided back into its traditional petty kingdoms, which left them vulnerable to the Norman invasion that swept Britain in 1066.

III

1. Yes, I love the *Casanova* movie with Heath Ledger.

2. Carnival is a Christian festival before Lent, usually in late February

or early March. Celebrations included feasts, street parties, parades, and other entertainments we today would associate with the circus. Costumes and masks are often a large part of celebrations. It's often a time of excessive consumption and indulgence before giving things up for Lent. Celebrations often include social satires (such as a reversal of the social castes), food fights, excessive drinking, sexual indulgences—basically, people took "Treat Yo'self" to heart and ran with it.

There was often concern about the excessive indulgence within the religious community, though it could also be seen as a healthy way to get all the sin out of people's systems before Lent.

3. Carnival in Venice sounded like a spectacle! Think modern-day Mardi Gras in New Orleans or Carnival in Rio. Venetian Carnival took place from the 12th century to 1797, when it was banned by the Austrian Emperor Francis II (Venice was taken by Napoleon that year and given over to Austria in the Treaty of Campo Formio). It took place intermittently over the next few centuries but more controlled and for specific feast days. It was reinstated in 1979 in an effort to revive Italian history and culture in the nation. The masks have since become an iconic symbol of Venice and Venetian Carnival, and one of the most popular contests held for the modern event is the Most Beautiful Mask Contest.

4. Venetian masks were an important part of Carnival and offered an extra layer of anonymity, so people could partake in all the social upheaval and celebrations. The famous Venetian mask that covers the top half of the face is a more modern invention. Traditional masks include the *bauta* (simple white mask with exaggerated noses and/or brows and no mouth), plague doctor's mask, and other stock character masks.

IV

1. Gavriel can be the god of my forest any day. That is all.

V

1. Lord Elgin was a real person: Thomas Bruce, 7th Earl of Elgin, of *that* Scottish Bruce family. He is infamous for his travels to Greece, where he'd originally planned to hire artists and drafters to draw and cast plasters of original Greek buildings, statues, and art in order to bring some culture back to Scotland (his thoughts not mine, I think Scotland has an abundance of culture). Rather than just bringing back copies, Elgin and his team instead brought back originals.

In a move that was controversial even in the early 1800s, Elgin brought back hundreds of marbles and other artwork from Greece to London from 1805–1812. Known as the Elgin Marbles, they were taken from their homeland and in some places even cut off buildings—most famously the pediment marbles from the Parthenon, one of the caryatids from the Erechtheion, and friezes from other temples of the Acropolis. Brought to London, Elgin had planned to open his own private museum. However, upon arriving home, he caught his wife Mary in the midst of an affair with Robert Ferguson, one of his oldest friends. Elgin and Mary went through a bitter divorce that nearly bankrupted him. Left with little means, and with the legality of the marbles' "acquisition" in question, the British government, through an act of Parliament, bought the collection from Elgin for less than half of what the venture had cost him over the years (honestly, good).

This collection was moved to the British Museum, where the marbles are still on display today. The Acropolis statuary has its own room in the museum. This is despite Greece wanting its heritage and culture back. Elgin claimed that the marbles were removed legally with the permission of an Ottoman (not Athenian or Greek) official in Athens (Greece at the time was a territory of the Ottoman Empire, centered in Turkey).

If the legality was suspish in the 1800s, I guarantee it wouldn't hold up today. Send the statues back to their home, where they belong.

2. Also, yes, I'm calling out empire waists. I'm sorry but in my experience, they aren't flattering for us plus-sized ladies with DDs.

VI

1. Yes, I love *The Phantom of the Opera*. No, I don't think Christine should've ended up with the Phantom, he's messy AF. Yes, the chandelier really did fall down in 1896. Electricity was added to the opera house in the mid-1890s and it's believed that the early wiring got too hot and melted the cables or that one of the counterbalances broke free. That it crashed during a performance is entirely my fancy. Let me have it!

The Palais Garnier was immortalized by both the novel and the musical *The Phantom of the Opera*. The chandelier crash inspired the scene in the novel when the Phantom makes off with Christine in the story's climax. It was the primary location for the Paris Opera and Ballet until a new building was opened in 1989.

VII

1. Neuschwanstein Castle was conceived and begun by Ludwig II of Bavaria in 1869. The king was an eccentric figure who spent large sums on lavish art and architecture projects. Neuschwanstein was built as a retreat for him. Deposed in 1886, the palace was never fully completed after Ludwig was removed. It remains an iconic landmark of Bavaria and southern Germany. And yes, it's the inspiration for Cinderella's Castle in Disneyland.

2. Among all the atrocities committed by the Nazis during WWII, the theft of much of Europe's cultural heritage (it's estimated the Nazis

stole and/or moved up to 20 percent of Europe's art) isn't the worst on their spectrum of terrible, but it was still pretty damn bad. Hitler considered himself an artist, and it was his vision to bring together all the best art of Europe to display in his ego pet project, the Führermuseum. It didn't matter that other nations, museums, and private citizens owned that art.

Much of the art and valuables stolen and seized by the Nazis came from the private collections of Jewish Europeans (such as, famously, the *Portrait of Adele Bloch-Bauer I* by Gustav Klimt). Almost immediately upon the occupation of France, Hitler and other interested Nazi elites like Hermann Goering started seizing the art they wanted. There are harrowing stories of people across Europe hiding or disguising their art, knowing Nazi raiders were coming. One of the bravest stories is that of Rose Valland, a Frenchwoman kept on by the Nazis to help catalog the art they stole, not realizing she spoke German. Rose took meticulous notes, which she handed over to Captain James Rorimer of the Monuments, Fine Arts, and Archives (MFAA) program, better known as the Monuments Men.

Rorimer himself was at Neuschwanstein Castle when Allied forces retook the region. Neuschwanstein acted as a repository for stolen art, especially what was stolen from France. The art was relatively safe there, as Neuschwanstein wasn't in an area at risk of attack because of its strategic insignificance. Before the Allies took the region, much of the most famous art was moved to underground locations, such as the salt mines at Altausee in Austria.

The MFAA worked throughout the war and after to conserve art and historical locations as well as repatriate stolen art and valuables. Not everything the Nazis stole has been recovered; there are 100,000 items still unaccounted for, most famously Raphael's Portrait of a Young Man. There are concerted efforts in particular to restore recovered art, valuables, and wealth to Jewish families.

3. The 53rd (Welsh) Infantry Division was a division of the British

Army during World Wars I and II. Made up primarily of men from western England and Wales, the 53rd participated in the liberation of France in 1944 and 1945. They took part in the Battle of the Bulge, the last major German offensive of the war in late 1944, and then were a major part of Operation Veritable. A pincer movement, Veritable was the northern arm that invaded the Reichswald ("Imperial Forest") region of Germany with the American Army moving in from the south. The 53rd took part in the month of fighting it took to clear the forest and sustained heavy casualties. Multiple sources talk about how brutal the fighting was, with German soldiers dug into bunkers and foxholes, fighting fervently now to defend their homeland. After taking the Reichswald, the 53rd moved south to help take the Hochwald ("High Forest") and into the southwest region of Germany. They participated in Operation Plunder, which saw the Allies cross the Rhine River into the German heartland. The division took part in postwar operations and was eventually disbanded.

VIII

1. Tuxedos, uniforms, and kilts are all well and good, but y'all. Fisherman (Aran) sweaters. I move to make this a new book boyfriend staple. Please join the club, it's very cozy. Authors, please write more fisherman sweater-wearing leading men. Thank you.

Glossary of People, Places, and Welsh Words

Albion—ancient, often poetic name for the island of Britain

Angles—Germanic tribe that invaded and settled eastern Britain in the 5th c.; their tribe and language is where we get the names England and English

Beltane—Celtic festival celebrated on May 1, the first day of summer

caer—castle, fort, fortress, especially of stone

Caerdyf—Cardiff, modern capital of Wales

Caer Gwyn—Carys and Gavriel's home, translates roughly to "Castle of Magic"

cariad—love, beloved, darling, sweetheart, lover

Cymru—Welsh name for Wales

Cymry—name of the Welsh people for themselves

Cynddylan—Early medieval Welsh prince and last ruler of Pengwern

Deganwy—medieval capital of Gwynedd

druid—religious leaders of Celtic society; soothsayers, healers, advisors

Eryri—traditional name for the region of Snowdonia in Wales

fae/fairy/faerie—supernatural beings often associated with nature, the underworld, and magic; thought to be the original peoples of Britain and Ireland; called the Tuatha De Danann in Irish folklore

ffyc—fuck

Fomorians—monstrous beings from Irish folklore, believed to be the ancient enemies of the Tuatha De Danann; they were sometimes described as giants or sea raiders

fy annwyl—my dear one, my darling

fy ffrind—my friend

fy nghariad—my love

Gorsedd—throne, mound of earth or barrow; a gathering of people, assembly; today references the Gorsedd Cymru, a society of Welsh poets and bards

Gruffydd ap Llywelyn—King of Wales from 1055–1063; first to unite all kingdoms of Wales under centralized leadership temporarily

gwiddon—witch, hag

Gwynedd—one of the largest and most powerful of the medieval Welsh petty kingdoms; traditionally held the northwest portion of modern Wales; includes the region of Eryri

Heledd—sister of Cynddylan, only survivor of the sack of Pengwern; narrator of the epic Welsh poem Canu Heledd

hiraeth—homesickness, nostalgia for the way things were, especially as it relates to Wales

offeiriad—priest, father

mo tè bhòidheach—(Scottish Gaelic) my pretty one

Morrígan—Celtic Irish goddess of battle, war, and fate; often depicted as a crow; portends doom and victory in battle

Pengwern—a smaller medieval Welsh petty kingdom or principality of Powys, believed to be in what is now east Wales and the English Midlands; destroyed around 658 by the Northumbrians

Powys—one of the larger of the medieval Welsh petty kingdoms; traditionally held the northeast portion of modern Wales and some of the English Midlands

Pritani—ancient name for the Celtic/Brittonic people of Great Britain

Rhiannon—magical female character of the Mabinogi, the earliest collection of Welsh prose stories; associated with horses and may be derived from an older Celtic or Gaullish horse goddess

Samhain—Celtic festival celebrated on October 31, last day of the harvest

Saxons—Germanic tribe that invaded and settled southeastern Britain in the 5th c.

Titania—one of several names attributed to the Fairy Queen, most famously by Shakespeare; the female ruler of the fae in medieval literature

Author's Note

Hi, all! Thank you all so much for reading my little novella. *Stone Hearts* began life as my contribution to the *I Am The Fire Charity Anthology* in 2022. All sales from that anthology were donated the National Network of Abortion Funds. I'm so excited now to release this story solo and hope you enjoyed all the extra scenes! The prologues were all incredibly self-indulgent. I wanted to write in certain time periods—and practice writing steamy scenes. Win win!

I loved getting to write all these historical places and periods, and let me tell you, 8 was the shortlist! I could definitely see myself doing more; there are so many awesome events our gargoyle cutie and broody fae could be at!

Stone Hearts stands on its own but starts off a series of interconnected standalones. Things start happening in that new gallery in San Francisco. The scene is set, and change is in the air! Carys and Gavriel have laid the groundwork for their clan, and now it's time to free the beasts!

The War of the Underhill series officially kicks off with book 1, *Heartsworn*, available now from Avon Books! Book 2, *Heartsworn*, arrives summer 2026.

Acknowledgements

I'd also like to take a moment to thank some of the people who made this book possible!

A huge thank you to Mita and Lexie, who first helped wrangle this story down to the needed word count. And Mita again for cleaning up my mess in the epilogues.

Thank you to Leah, my awesome PA, who helped me go from hobbyist to big girl author with my own website and everything.

And I have to mention too the amazing artists who helped bring Carys and Gavriel to life. A huge thank you to Beth Gilbert, the stunningly talented artist who illustrated the cover. I also want to thank Jeannine, Diana, and more, you're all so amazing and I'm so grateful for the care you've taken with my book babies!

Other Works

A Time of War and Demons (House of the Rising Sun, Book 1), fantasy romance novel

Aerie (Broken Wings Duet, Book 1), fantasy romance novel
Haven (Broken Wings Duet, Book 2), fantasy romance novel

Stone Hearts (War of the Underhill, Book 0), historical monster/fantasy romance novella
Heartsong (War of the Underhill, Book 1), monster/paranormal romance novel, February 2026
Heartsworn (War of the Underhill, Book 2), monster/paranormal romance novel, October 2026

Halfling (Monstrous World, Book 1), monster/fantasy romance novel
Ironling (Monstrous World, Book 2), monster/fantasy romance novel
Sweetling (Monstrous World, Book 3), fae/fantasy romance novel
Faeling (Monstrous World, Book 4), monster/fae/fantasy romance novel
Changelings (Monstrous World, Book 5), monster/fantasy romance novella collection, Autumn 2025 + Spring 2026
Foundling (Monstrous World, Book 6), monster/fae/fantasy romance, Summer 2026

Stay in Touch

If you'd like to stay in touch, come on over to socials and say hi! I'm around on most platforms as se.wendel.author, and I'm most active on Instagram. Come check it out to find out about what I'm working on, get some reading recommendations, and get spammed with pictures of my cat. What's not to love?

You can also check out all my books, commissioned art, and book merch shop on my author website (www.sewendelauthor.com)! Lots of good stuff over there!

I've also started up a monthly newsletter. The first is out now and you can subscribe on my website to keep up with me and my news.